Paige released a sigh.

"Thank God. I was so worried about you, but I didn't call 911 and we're on our way to a safe house."

Paige waited for Asher to say more, maybe how he felt or what he thought happened to him.

Instead, he downed the water and gazed out the window.

"Asher?" He seemed awake but was this some kind of suspended state of consciousness? She waited for several minutes that stretched into an eternity.

"Asher? Did you hear me? We're on our way to a safe house." She touched his cool hand.

He snatched his hand away from her, screwed on the lid to the empty bottle, placed it back in the cup holder and finally turned toward her, his green eyes dark and unfathomable.

"When the hell were you going to tell me about our daughter?"

DELTA FORCE DADDY

CAROL ERICSON

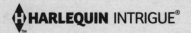

Recycling programs
for this product may
not exist in your area.

ISBN-13: 978-1-335-52679-3

Delta Force Daddy

Copyright © 2018 by Carol Ericson

Printed in U.S.A.

www.Harlequin.com

Carol Ericson is a bestselling, award-winning author of more than forty books. She has an eerie fascination for true-crime stories, a love of film noir and a weakness for reality TV, all of which fuel her imagination to create her own tales of murder, mayhem and mystery. To find out more about Carol and her current projects, please visit her website at www.carolericson.com, "where romance flirts with danger."

Visit the Author Profile page at Harlequin.com.

CAST OF CHARACTERS

Paige Sterling—A therapist who specializes in PTSD, she has her most important client ever—her Delta Force fiancé, who was ambushed and injured by the enemy. She not only has to help him remember what happened at the meeting he attended with his commander, Major Denver, that resulted in the major going AWOL, she has to help him remember her and their child.

Asher Knight—This Delta Force soldier can't remember what happened the moment he got injured and his commander went AWOL, but he knows there's something suspicious about his "rehabilitation." Although he has a visceral attraction to the woman who rescues him, he soon learns even she is keeping secrets from him.

Ivy Knight—Paige and Asher's daughter, she becomes a pawn in a dangerous political game.

Dylan Curran—An army ranger who was at the meeting with Asher and Major Denver, he paid an even higher price than Asher for his involvement in Major Denver's secret meeting.

Tabitha Crane—A nurse who helped Asher in his rehabilitation, she now has a dangerous obsession with him that could get them both killed.

"Linc"—While sent to kill Asher, he learns he may be just as expendable as his target.

Frankie "The Greek" Greco—A mobster with a soft heart, he's a friend of Asher's imprisoned father and indebted to him; now Asher just might have to call in a few favors.

Major Rex Denver—Framed for working with a terrorist group, the Delta Force commander has gone AWOL and is on the run, but he knows he's onto a larger plot and that he can count on his squad to have his back and help clear his name.

Prologue

Pain seared through his left ankle as he put weight on it. He listed to the side, throwing out a hand to wedge it against the rocky wall of the cliff face. As the gritty surface abraded the skinned flesh on the heel of his hand, he sucked in a breath.

Sinking into a crouch, he extended his injured leg in front of him and surveyed the rocky expanse below. Even with two steady legs, hydrated and nourished, this landscape would pose a challenge to navigate. Parched, weakened by hunger and with a bum ankle, he didn't stand a chance.

He eyed the gray skies, scuffs of cloud rolling across the expanse, promising rain and relief—and more challenges. He dragged his boot over the rocks coated with dirt. Once the rains started, rivulets of water would wash the grit from the stones, joining forces in a muddy stream, making his path to the bottom of the mountain a slippery—and dangerous— proposition.

He'd already witnessed one of his men take a tumble down the side of a mountain. Had Knight survived that fall? If he knew anything about his Delta Force team, he'd lay odds on it. But even if Asher Knight had made it through, the men who had double-crossed them would've finished off Knight.

They wouldn't have left any witnesses.

He took a deep breath and swiped the back of his hand across his mouth. "Did you think it was gonna be easy going AWOL in Afghanistan in the middle of enemy territory, Denver?"

His voice sounded rusty to his own ears, but it was strong enough to startle a bird from its hiding place. The bird scuttled and flapped before taking wing and soaring up to those threatening clouds. He watched its ascent with something like envy roiling in his gut.

He willed himself to stand up—he owed it to Knight and the others to persevere. He stomped his bad foot and secured the laces on his boot—the tighter, the better for support. He hoisted his backpack and belted it around his waist. He strapped his rifle across his body. Couldn't afford to lose that if he took a fall.

The first step jolted his bones, and he gritted his teeth. The next step felt worse, but at least he didn't slide down the mountain.

Several more yards of jerky movement and his face broke into a sweat, which dripped into his eyes, blurring his vision. Maybe this descent would work better by touch and feel than sight, anyway. He didn't need to see the view if he pitched off a cliff.

Something scrabbled behind him, dislodging several small stones that tumbled down and peppered the back of his legs. He could get lucky and ride down with an avalanche.

"Meester."

Ripping his sidearm from its holster, he whipped around and took aim at…a boy. The boy looked down at him from several feet above, clinging to the side of the mountain like a goat.

Denver's muscles coiled, and he spat out in guttural Pashto, "Who are you? Where did you come from?"

The boy's eyes grew round, crowding out the other features in his gaunt face. Then he raised an old Russian rifle, pointed it at him and said, "American soldier. You die today."

Chapter One

"I'm sorry. Lieutenant Knight doesn't remember you." The army officer on the line cleared his throat. "But he doesn't remember much of anything. He didn't mention your name. That's for sure. Are you positive you're engaged to him?"

Paige's hand shook as she tried to hold on to her phone. "That's crazy. Do you think I'd make up some phony engagement to an injured Delta Force soldier?"

The army officer on the line paused, and a burning rage sizzled through Paige's veins. She released it as a hiss through her teeth.

"I—I'm sure you are engaged and Lieutenant Knight will remember soon enough. The doctors are confident he'll remember everything."

"Oh, that's encouraging." Paige took a deep breath and closed her eyes. "What else has he forgotten?"

"Well, ma'am." The officer coughed. "If he's forgotten it, how would he be able to tell us about it?"

Her fist clenched in her lap. "You must know details of his life. Does he remember them?"

"I'm just the messenger, ma'am. I don't know much about Lieutenant Knight's condition."

That's for sure. Paige took a gulp of water from the glass on her desk. "Can I talk to his doctors? I'm a psychologist myself."

"Ma'am, since you're not next of kin, the doctors won't speak to you."

She ground her back teeth together, suppressing the scream that ached in her throat. "His mother is dead, his father's in prison and he's an only child. Whom exactly is the doctor speaking to about his care?"

"I don't know, ma'am. We called you because Lieutenant Knight had your name and number in his phone. Yours was the only number listed in his favorites."

"There!" She was his favorite. Didn't that mean something? "Obviously, I'm the person he'd want you to contact in an emergency. Can I fly out to see him?"

"No, ma'am. We can't allow that—yet."

The soldier's words punched her in the gut, and she doubled over. She had to speak to Asher, had to see him. Once they were back in each other's arms, he'd remember everything.

"How much longer will he be in Germany?"

"Again, ma'am, I'm not at liberty to discuss any of the particulars of the lieutenant's recovery with you. I got the order to call you out of courtesy…because you're a favorite."

She wished he'd stop saying that word. "Can you

at least tell me he's not badly injured physically? Will he make a full recovery?"

"He's strong. As far as I know, he's doing fine physically and is expected to make a full recovery. And, ma'am?"

"Yes?"

"That's off the record."

When the call ended, Paige sank to her chair behind the desk and placed her hands flat on the surface. What did this mean? Just because Asher had amnesia and couldn't recall the details of their relationship...or her, did that mean it never happened? What were those doctors in Germany doing to help him recover his memories?

A light blinked above her door, indicating her next client had arrived. How in the world could she help anyone right now when she couldn't even help herself?

She dragged herself out of the chair, straightened her shoulders and strode to the door. Plastering a smile on her face, she swung it open.

"Come on in, Krystal."

Her next client sashayed into the room, flicking her long hair over one shoulder and wiggling her hips in a tight skirt that she must wear to impress her johns—which she wasn't supposed to have anymore.

She smacked a piece of paper on Paige's desk and tapped it with one long fingernail. "Can you sign now? Only two more sessions after this one before I satisfy the terms of my probation."

Paige scribbled her signature on the form. "I hope

you've gotten more out of these sessions than just the completion of your probation."

"I have." Krystal sat in her usual chair and crossed her long legs. "You've been great, Paige."

Paige took the seat across from Krystal and nodded, which Krystal took as a signal to launch into a recitation of her sad life story.

Her words filled the room, and Paige tried to catch one or two to get the gist, although she'd heard most of it before.

"So, do you think I should call my father?"

Paige blinked and dropped the pencil she'd been tapping against the arm of her chair. She dipped forward and patted the carpet to buy time, to hide her confusion at the question that seemed to have come out of left field.

"It's right next to the leg."

"Huh?" Paige looked up, her face flushed with heat.

"The pencil. It's next to the left chair leg."

Paige's fingers inched to the left and curled around the pencil. "Got it."

Krystal arched one painted-on eyebrow. "So, do you? Do you think I should call the scumbag?"

Clearing her throat, Paige folded her hands in her lap. "What do you think?"

"I knew you were going to say that." Krystal slumped in her chair and clicked together her decorated nails. "Why do you always answer a question with a question?"

"If you did call your father, what would you say?"

"I'm not sure." Krystal chewed all the lipstick off her bottom lip. "I don't want to remember any more stuff about him."

"Any more stuff?"

"I know you helped me with the repressed memories and all that, and remembering my father's abuse really did help me deal with my issues and figure out why I thought hooking was a good way to make a living, but I think there might be more." Krystal dashed a tear from her face, leaving a black streak on her cheek. "I have a funny feeling in my gut that he did more to me, and I'm afraid seeing him again is gonna make those memories bubble up. And I don't want them. I don't want them anymore."

Paige hunched forward, her knees almost touching Krystal's, and shoved a box of tissues at her. "You want me to tell you what to do? Screw it. Don't talk to him. Don't see him."

After Krystal left her office, all smiles and thanks, Paige plopped down in her desk chair and scooted up to her computer. She brought up her calendar on the monitor and placed her first call to cancel her appointments for the next two weeks.

If just seeing her father would prompt memories for Krystal, maybe seeing her would do the same for Asher.

She felt guilty canceling on her clients, but she'd just gotten her most important client ever.

ASHER WEDGED HIS boots against the railing surrounding the porch and squinted into the woods beyond the clearing. The doctors here must be wary of him going postal or something, because he could sense them spying on him. Spying? That was what his intuition told him, anyway.

He huffed out a breath and watched it form a cloud in the cold air. Funny how he could remember all the skills he'd learned as a Delta Force member, including that last mission—the one that had thrown him for a loop and wiped out all his previous memories—but he couldn't recall the rest of his life.

The doctors had assured him it would all come back, not that he had much of a family to come back to—mother dead, father in federal prison for bank robbery and no siblings or even aunts and uncles. No wife.

He glanced at his left ring finger and wiggled it. No ring tan and the docs had assured him they'd perused his army files and no wife was listed—even though it felt like he could have one. Something—or someone—more than just his memories felt missing.

The guys who might know more about him than anyone else—his Delta Force team—couldn't be reached right now. Their commander, Major Rex Denver, had gone AWOL. He should know—he'd been there the moment Denver had escaped.

The man he'd trusted with his life, had looked up to, had followed blindly, that man had shot and killed an army ranger and had pushed Asher over the edge of a cliff before escaping. Asher had been rescued by a squad of army rangers, surviving the fall with minor injuries…because his head had taken the brunt of the impact.

Asher ran a fingertip along the scar on the back of his head where his hair had yet to grow back. That moment, that scene when Denver had shot the ranger and then turned on him and pushed him into oblivion was etched on his brain, but he couldn't remember his own family.

The doctors in Germany had tried to fill him in on his background, so he knew the outline, hadn't even been shocked by the details of a dead mother and a father imprisoned for bank robbery. On some gut level that life had resonated with him, but he couldn't recall the specifics.

The docs showed him pictures of his Delta Force teammates, had even allowed him a phone call with Cam, who'd been on leave.

Asher scratched the edges of his scar. That phone call hadn't gone well. Cam had accused him of lying. He didn't have a chance to get into it with him because the psychologist ended the call. The doc had shrugged off Cam as a hothead, and that definitely rang a bell with Asher.

An ache creeped up his neck, and Asher tried to massage it away. The doctors had warned him about trying too hard to remember, but what else could he do in this convalescent home? The army called it a rehabilitation center, but Asher didn't feel rehabilitated. He needed…something. He couldn't put his finger on it, but a big piece of his life was missing.

He snorted and dropped his feet from the railing,

his boots thumping against the wood porch. *Most* of his life was missing right now, and if he wanted it back, he'd be well-advised to keep taking his meds and going to his sessions with the shrinks. Shrink. Shrinky-dinky.

Where had that come from? He shook his throbbing head. The stuff that popped into his mind sometimes convinced him he'd already gone off the deep end.

A flash of light glinted from the trees, and Asher squinted. As far as he knew, no roads ran through that part of the property. A new symptom, flashes of light, had probably just been added to his repertoire of strange happenings in his brain.

He rubbed his eyes, and the light flickered again, glinting in the weak winter sunlight. He cranked his head around to survey the buildings behind him. Most of the patients here napped after lunch and the staff took the time to relax. He had the place to himself—as long as his spies were on break.

When the third flash of light made its way out of the dense forest, Asher pushed back from his chair and stretched. Investigating this would take his mind off the jumble in his brain.

He zipped up his jacket and stuffed his hands into his pockets. This felt like a mission and his fingertips buzzed, but he felt stripped bare without his weapon. He wouldn't need it for what would probably turn out to be something caught on the branches of a tree, but at least he had a mission.

He strode across the rolling lawn, scattered with

chairs and chaise lounges, abandoned in the wintry chill of December. He glanced over his shoulder, expecting someone to stop him, although he didn't know why. He wasn't a prisoner here. Was he?

Hunching his shoulders, he made a beeline for the forest at the edge of the grass. When he reached the tree line, he tensed his muscles. His instincts, which seemed to have been suppressed by the drugs he got on a regular basis, flared into action.

He stepped onto the thick floor of the wooded area, his boots crunching pine needles. Where had the light gone? It had flashed just once more on his trek across the lawn, like a beacon guiding him.

The rustle of a soft footstep had him jerking to his right, his hand reaching impotently for a gun. "Come out where I can see you."

A hint of blue appeared amid the unrelenting greens and browns of the forest, and then a head, covered with a hood, popped out from behind the trunk of a tree.

"Asher?"

He swallowed and blinked. Had the docs chased him out here, too?

The figure emerged from behind the tree and the hood fell back. A tumble of golden hair spilled over the woman's shoulder, and Asher had a strange urge to run his fingers through the silky strands.

"Asher, it's me." She held out a hand, keeping one arm around the trunk of the tree and leaning out toward the side as if approaching a wild animal. "It's Paige. Do you remember?"

Paige? Her voice sounded like cool water tumbling over rocks in a stream. A sharp pain lanced the wound on his head, and he rubbed his fingers along the scar to make it stop.

She hugged the tree with one arm, her other arm stretched out toward him in a yearning gesture that made his heart ache.

"Are you in pain, my love?"

His mouth gaped open. "I-is this a joke?"

Her eye twitched, but her smooth face remained impassive. "No joke, Asher. I'm your fiancée."

"My fiancée? But…"

A million emotions coursed through his brain in a tangled mess. *Ivy. Shrinky-dinky.* He tried to latch on to one, but something stung the back of his neck. As he clapped his hand against his flesh, the beautiful face before him melted away and he sank into darkness.

Chapter Two

As Asher hit the ground, Paige gasped and lurched forward.

Loud voices and a crashing noise had her jumping back behind the tree.

"What the hell, Granger? Did you have to shoot him with a dart?"

Paige backed up and scrambled for cover behind a clump of bushes and a rotting log. She flipped up her hood and smashed her face into the mulch, the smell of moist, verdant dirt filling her nostrils.

"Don't give me that, Lewis. If that guy gets away, it's your ass and my ass."

"I don't think he was running for the hills or anything. Where would he be going? Besides, he's got enough drugs pumping through his veins that he wouldn't get far, anyway."

Paige held her breath as two sets of footsteps marched closer to her hiding place. She couldn't see the two men and she hoped to God they couldn't see her.

The other man, Granger, snorted. "You're gonna

count on that? This dude's big, and even though his mind's messed up, he's still in Delta Force physical condition."

"That's exactly my point." The underbrush crackled and rustled as if the two men were hauling a tree trunk. "You brought him down, and now we gotta carry him back. We coulda just told him the Ping-Pong tournament was starting or something."

A bug crawled across Paige's face and she squeezed her eyes closed, willing it away from her nose. These two men could not catch her here, as much as she wanted to save Asher from their clutches.

"We didn't know what he was up to or his state of mind. I don't trust any of these guys, and I'm not gonna lose my job or risk getting my ass kicked by any of them—especially this one."

Huffs, puffs and curses replaced the conversation of the two men, and when the forest had gone silent once again, Paige raised her head and peeked over the crest of the log.

She crawled on her belly in the opposite direction, every cell in her body screaming at her to turn back toward Asher. Would he remember their meeting when he came to? Would he understand what they'd done to him? Would he know to keep her a secret?

By the time she reached the end of the wooded area and scrambled downhill to the access road, tears streamed down her face. What were they doing to Asher and why?

He was a hero who'd risked his life for his country, and that very country now held him captive, held his mind captive.

She hiked along the side of the access road, her boots scuffing the dirt. She couldn't go to the police. She couldn't go to the army. She might be putting Asher in danger if she did.

Before she hit the main road, she glanced over her shoulder at the hillside covered with trees. She'd be back.

She'd be back to get Asher and get him the hell out of that loony bin—after all, she was the fiancée of a D-Boy.

ASHER GROANED AND shifted to his side. His tongue swept his bottom lip and he tasted dirt. The forest. The woman.

A chipper voice pierced his brain. "Coming to?"

He peeled open one eye and took in the form of a sturdy nurse in pink scrubs. It wasn't this woman— Tabitha—he'd seen in the forest. How come he could remember her so well?

"What happened?" He cupped the back of his head with his hand, flattening his palm against the scar.

"You got a little too ambitious." She shook a finger at him and he wanted to chomp it off, but the sentiment floated away before it even registered.

"While everyone else was napping, you decided to take a walk across the lawn and collapsed midway."

Asher ground his teeth together, mashing the dirt in his mouth. *You're lying, Tabitha.*

"I remember heading across the grass." He massaged his temple with two fingers. "I don't remember much after that."

As he struggled to sit up, Nurse Tabitha sprang into action and perched on the edge of the bed. "Let me."

She curled a strong arm around his shoulders, hooked the other around his chest and helped him sit up. "There."

"How'd I get back here?" He straightened up farther, hoping to dislodge her hand resting on his chest.

She curled her fingers, briefly digging her nails into his pec before releasing him. "Granger and Lewis went out to move the lawn furniture and saw you sprawled on the grass. They got you back to your room."

Asher ran his tongue along his dry teeth and recognized the cotton mouth associated with the meds they gave him—the meds he'd chucked this morning. His gaze wandered to the window, the curtains open to the dark night.

"Did I pass out? Have a seizure? It was daytime when I took that walk, or at least late afternoon."

Tabitha's translucent eyelashes fluttered. "Just a little overexertion, and because of your…brain injury, the doctors thought it best to medicate you."

Of course they did.

Asher scratched the scruff on his jaw. "Thank God for Lewis and…"

"Granger."

"Right."

Tabitha hunched forward, her pink tongue darting out of her mouth. "I could shave you if you'd like."

He'd rather grow a beard down to his knees. "I'm…"

"How's the patient feeling, Tabitha?"

The nurse leaned forward and pressed a warm, clammy hand against his forehead. "He's awake and feeling fine, certainly looking fine, and I'm sure he's ready to eat. Are you hungry, Lieutenant?"

Asher threw back the covers, realizing for the first time he was naked beneath a hospital gown that gaped open in the front. Who'd done the honors of taking off his clothes? He sure hoped it wasn't Nurse Touchy-Feely.

His gaze darted around the room, looking for his missing clothes. "I am ready to eat. Too late to grab something in the mess hall?"

"Not so fast there, Lieutenant Knight." Dr. Evans stood by the bed, hovering over him. "I'd like to run a few tests and then bring Dr. Goshen in to see you."

"The shrink?" He swung his legs over the side of the bed, almost taking out Tabitha. "I'm fine. I passed out. I didn't have a hallucination."

Did he? Was Paige, his fiancée, all an illusion? Nobody had said anything yet about finding a woman in the woods. If she hadn't been a dream, he hoped she got away, because he had a feeling she wouldn't be welcome here.

"Your passing out could've been psychological. We don't want to take any chances." The doctor jerked his thumb at Tabitha. "While we're poking and prodding your body and mind, Tabitha can go down to the kitchen and put in an order for your dinner." The doctor adjusted his glasses. "You can have dinner in bed and we'll give you something to ensure you have a good night's sleep."

Asher's blood boiled and his hand clenched into a fist. Then he closed his eyes, dragging in a deep breath. If he kicked up a ruckus now, they'd never let him out of their sights again.

"You know, that sounds good about now."

"Of course it does. Tabitha, help the lieutenant back into bed. I'll do my thing and go round up Dr. Goshen."

Tabitha reached across him, her right breast brushing his arm, and fluffed up his pillows. "We had some delicious pork chops and mashed potatoes tonight. I'll have the cook fix you up a special plate and have him add an extra dessert."

"That'll work." He eased back onto the bed, his gown hitching up to his thighs.

Tabitha tugged on the edge of the material, her fingers dangerously close to his crotch, and then twitched the covers back over his legs. She tucked the covers around his waist, and her hands lingered next to his hips.

"Anything else I can get you before ordering your dinner?"

"I'm fine, Tabitha. Thanks." He even managed to crack a smile in her direction.

Wrong move.

The nurse turned pink up to her strawberry blond

hair. "We're going to make sure you stay that way...
Asher."

When Dr. Evans returned with the psychiatrist,
Dr. Goshen, Tabitha squeezed Asher's thigh and gave
him an encouraging nod.

He endured their invasion of his body and mind
with a smile on his face and an agreeable tone in his
voice. When Tabitha returned with a tray groaning
with steaming food, Dr. Goshen shook out two blue
pills next to the plate.

"Take these when you get some food in your stomach, and you'll be back on track."

Back on track to crazy town? The only track he
wanted to be on was the one back to the forest...
and Paige.

PAIGE RAN HER fingers through her damp hair and
collapsed on the hotel bed. He really didn't know
her. His dark green eyes had been vacant when he
looked at her. Maybe he suffered from more than
memory loss.

She'd worked with enough people suffering from
PTSD to know it could take many forms. Maybe
he was a danger to himself and others and that was
why the army had him stashed away here—captive.
Maybe he'd been trying to go AWOL, like Major
Denver. Maybe they were just holding him here until
he got better before they court-martialed him.

She rolled over onto her stomach and pounded the
pillow with her fist. No way. She had a hard time be-
lieving Major Denver turned, but apparently Asher

himself had confirmed it. He'd been the lone survivor of the disastrous mission that had resulted in the death of an army ranger, the defection of Denver and Asher's fall and subsequent amnesia.

If Asher were in trouble with the army, wouldn't they just tell her? That would be enough to keep her away. Her inside army source, Dad's friend and now Mom's confidant Terrence Elder, hadn't mentioned anything about an arrest or court-martial. Terrence had pulled in a few favors to find out where Asher had been sent after Germany. That was how Paige had tracked Asher down to the convalescent facility, Hidden Hills, here in Vermont.

Asher's own teammates had been no help at all. If they'd returned her calls, and only a few did, they denied any knowledge of Asher's whereabouts and weren't too concerned about finding him. They'd viewed his accusations against Major Denver as the supreme betrayal of the man and the team.

But Asher would always do the right thing. With his father in federal prison for bank robbery, Asher followed the straight and narrow path. If he saw any wrongdoing, he'd report it—no matter who it was or how much it pained him to do so. She had firsthand knowledge of that.

If Asher said Major Denver killed that army ranger, pushed Asher off a cliff and took off, that was what happened.

But Asher had amnesia. How did he remember all that and not remember his fiancée? And if he didn't remember her, he didn't remember...

Her cell phone rang on the nightstand and she swept it off and answered. "Hi, Mom. Everything okay?"

"We're fine. Everything okay there? Did you see him?"

"Sort of. It's a long story." She tapped her phone's display. "You're not using FaceTime. Is Ivy still awake? It's three hours earlier there."

"I'm sorry, honey. Ivy went down for a nap right after dinner. Do you want me to do the face thing when she wakes up?"

"That's all right, Mom. I'm exhausted."

"I-is Asher okay? Do you think you can help him?"

Paige scooped in a big breath. "I do. I think I can help him."

"All by yourself? Maybe you should come home, Paige. You don't need this stress. Let the army handle it."

"I can handle the stress, Mom. Don't worry about me. It's Asher who needs help this time, and I'm not going to abandon him."

Her mother clicked her tongue. "Don't push yourself. You don't do well under pressure."

After that comment, Paige ended her call with Mom sooner rather than later and stretched out on the bed, staring at the ceiling.

She'd better start doing well under pressure, because the only way to help Asher was to get him out of that hellhole and restore his memory of her...and their daughter.

THE NEXT MORNING after breakfast, Paige shook out a clean pair of jeans. She'd wear the same hooded jacket as yesterday, since it seemed to have kept her hidden in the forest. Those two goons had no idea she was hiding in plain sight.

Asher had been on that porch by himself after lunch, so she'd aim for the same time again. Would he follow her signal? Would he rat her out—just like he'd ratted out Denver?

At least nobody had come into the small town of Mooseville looking for her. If she could get back to that wooded area again, she'd be safe. She just needed Asher to trust her.

Could he trust a…stranger? She clutched the jeans to her chest and bowed her head. She and Asher could never be strangers. Her love for him soaked every pore in her body.

When he found out she was pregnant, he'd swept her up in his arms and swung her around and around, even though the pregnancy had been a surprise and she wasn't quite…ready. He'd wanted nothing more than a family of his own…and now he couldn't even remember he had one.

She wiped the back of her hand across her tingling nose. She had no time for tears and no time for Mom's doubts. She had to rescue her man, if he'd let her.

After lunch, Paige parked her rental car in a turn-off on the main road, tucking it away and out of sight. As she hiked up the road to the access trail, she tilted back her head and studied the sky. The sun still shone through the clouds, enough for her to catch its beams with her mirror and signal Asher, as she'd done yesterday.

She ducked onto the access road and pumped her legs up the hill as the terrain grew more challenging. A steep angle and a few bushes didn't faze her. She'd hike through fire and brimstone to get to Asher.

The trees became denser, but Paige had marked her way the day before and those bits of blue yarn guided her back toward the compound perched on the hill.

She located her lookout tree and jumped to catch the lowest branch. She swung herself up and clambered from branch to branch like a clumsy monkey to reach her perch.

She shrugged off her pack and pulled out the binoculars. She scanned the desolate lawn. Maybe the action perked up in the warmer weather months... or maybe this retreat kept its patients drugged up and chained in the basement. Clenching her teeth, she shivered.

Fifteen minutes later Asher rewarded her patience by appearing on the porch, taking the same chair as yesterday. She focused the lenses on him, and her heart filled with joy. He looked healthy, if... lackadaisical.

As she reached into the inside pocket of her jacket, the door behind Asher opened and a nurse stepped onto the porch.

"Damn." Paige's whisper stirred the leaves on the branch hanging next to her face.

Were they watching him now? They must've been watching him yesterday to notice he'd left the porch and loped across the grass.

Her jaw ached with tension and disappointment. She might just have to go through the front door and demand to see him.

She refocused on Asher and the nurse and pressed her lips into a thin line. Was personal massage part of Asher's recovery?

The nurse, standing behind him, had her hands on his shoulders, massaging and rubbing him. Each time she reached forward, her hands slid beneath his jacket and moved against his chest.

Either Asher liked it or he was too zoned out to care. Each time the nurse's hands slid farther and farther down his chest, working toward the inevitable happy ending.

Asher turned his head and said something, and she stopped. Had he gotten the feeling his fiancée was watching?

When the nurse retreated inside, Paige grabbed the mirror and caught the weak sun. She tilted it back and forth, and Asher raised his head.

He'd seen it.

Paige's soaring spirits crashed a minute later when Nurse Grabby-Hands returned to the scene, this time pushing a wheelchair ahead of her.

Paige held her breath as the nurse helped Asher from the chair to the wheelchair. He listed to the side, and the large woman wrapped both of her arms around his body to right him. She kept her arms around him, putting her face close to his while talking to him.

Paige growled. "Get out of his face."

The nurse tucked a blanket around his legs and aimed the chair down the ramp.

If Asher needed a blanket on his lap, he'd be too weak to accompany her through the forest and down the hill. Squinting into the binoculars, Paige tracked their progress across the lawn. The nurse pushed the chair with one hand, her other resting on Asher's shoulder.

They made it about midway and stopped. Paige swore when she noticed Asher's attire. He did have a jacket on against the cold, but he wore it over a hospital gown. No wonder he had a blanket draped over his lower extremities. He was in bigger trouble than Paige imagined and a sob burst from her chest. She'd never get him out of here like that…especially with Nurse Ratched hovering over him.

Suddenly both of their heads jerked in unison. The nurse turned to face the building with the porch where Asher had been sitting.

Paige swept her binoculars toward the building and zeroed in on a doctor standing and waving. Paige tracked back to Asher and the nurse on the grass. The nurse jumped to her feet and waved back.

Leaning over Asher, the nurse smoothed the blanket across Asher's lap and tucked it under his thighs. Then she ran her hands over his chest before pulling his jacket closed. Finally, she turned and scurried back to the building.

Paige watched the doctor and nurse team go inside and shut the door behind them. She jerked the binoculars back to Asher and held the mirror up to the sun again, tilting it back and forth.

But what could he do in a gown and a blanket? He didn't even have shoes.

Asher sat quietly for several moments, and then Paige's heart slammed against her chest as he rose from the wheelchair. The blanket fell from his lap and he bunched it up and stuffed it into the chair. Then he shrugged out of the jacket and wrapped it around the blanket. From behind and from a distance, it might just look like someone slumped over in the chair.

Without looking behind him once, Asher took off in a jog across the lawn.

Paige stashed the binoculars in her backpack and scrambled down the tree. She hit the thick carpet of mulch just as she heard Asher crash through the trees.

"Are you here? Are you here? Paige?"

Her heart took flight. He remembered her. All he needed was to see her once.

"Here! I'm here!"

He emerged through the trees, the hospital gown flapping around his bare legs, a pair of socks the only barrier between his feet and the sharp needles and twigs that formed the forest floor.

She rushed to him. "Asher. Oh my God, Asher."

He grabbed her hands and held her off from throwing herself in his arms.

"You've gotta help me. You've gotta get me out of this place…whoever you are."

Chapter Three

His words chipped off a piece of her heart, but she squared her shoulders and stepped back from him. "We have to go through these woods and down a steep hill. Can you make it dressed like that?"

"I could make it naked with one arm tied behind my back to get out of here. Lead the way."

"Let's go. You should've kept that jacket though."

"That jacket might buy me some time if someone happens to look out the window at the drugged-out invalid to make sure he's still drooling in his chair."

"You're not drugged?"

"I've been spitting them out—and pretending."

She held a branch to the side for him. "They still didn't trust you enough to give you clothes."

"They underestimated me." He charged after her. "Don't worry about clearing a path for me. Just go. I'll follow you."

"Your physical health is okay?"

"Strong as an ox." He nudged her back. "Stop talking. You're wasting energy."

She scrabbled and stumbled her way to the forest's

edge. When they reached the path down to the access road, she made a half turn. "You can make it down?"

"I survived a tumble off a mountain in Afghanistan. I can traverse a wooded hill in Vermont."

He didn't need her to show him the way anymore, and he barreled past her into the descent, reaching back with one hand. "Keep up now."

As his gown gaped open in the back, her eyebrows shot up. "You're naked under that thing."

"Their way of keeping me tame. Like I said. They underestimated me." He craned his head over his shoulder. "If you're really my fiancée like you said, my bare backside shouldn't shock you."

"I'm not shocked." She twisted her fingers out of his grasp. "And stop dragging me or we'll both end up in a freefall to the bottom of this hill."

They had no words left as they negotiated their way down. When they hit the access road, Asher peeled off his socks, now decorated with dirt, small pebbles and pine needles.

He bunched them in his hand and stuffed them into the pack on her back. "I don't want to leave any evidence."

He hung back as the access road spilled onto the main drag. "It's too exposed here."

"The car's less than half a mile away. Wait here and I'll pick you up."

As she started to turn away, he grabbed her hand. "You'll be back?"

"I didn't come all the way out here to leave you

behind, Asher Knight…even if you don't know who the hell I am."

Paige ran to the car, the pack jostling on her back. She wished she had some clothes in there for Asher. She never would've imagined she'd be rescuing him in a hospital gown and nothing else.

When she reached the car, she lunged at the door and threw it open. She gunned the engine and swung into a wide U-turn.

The empty road in front of the access entrance stretched before her, and a wave of panic washed through her body. When Asher stepped out from behind a bush, a sob escaped from Paige's lips.

"Get hold of yourself, girl." She flipped a U-turn again and pulled over.

Before she even stopped the car, Asher had yanked at the door and jumped inside. "Go!"

She didn't have to be told twice—or even once. Her foot punched the accelerator and the little rental roared in protest before switching gears and lurching forward.

The tires ate up the road, and Asher put a hand on her arm. "Slow down. We don't want to get a ticket."

Glancing in the rearview mirror, she eased off the gas. "But if we do get pulled over, we can tell the police what's going on. You're not a prisoner. You haven't been committed."

"Really?" He cocked an eyebrow at her. "I don't know what the hell is going on right now. That's the US Army, the United States government. They can tell the cops whatever they want and, I guarantee you, I'll be back in their clutches."

Paige's heart flip-flopped, and she tried to swallow her fear. She was the daughter of a police officer, had always trusted law enforcement, had always trusted authority. Now she had to rely on herself.

Asher jerked his head toward her and braced his hands against the dashboard. "Unless that's what you want? Where are you taking me?"

Paige drew in her bottom lip. Great. Now she had to deal with Asher's paranoia. Was it real or imagined? She slid a sideways gaze at him. Maybe his mental issues involved more than amnesia. Maybe he'd been kept naked and drugged because he *did* pose a threat to himself…and others.

She could feel his hard stare boring into the side of her face. A stranger's stare.

"Is that it? Are you one of them?"

His harsh voice grated against her ear, and she took a deep breath. If he could listen to reason and think logically, that would tell her a lot about his mental state.

"I'm taking you to my motel right now. We should leave as soon as I can check out. This is a small town and the people at that house of horrors will most likely fan out there first to look for you."

He nodded, his mouth still tight.

"Why would I contact you secretly and help you escape if I were in cahoots with the hospital and planned to deliver you back to them? What would be the plan? To test you? They don't need to test you.

They have you captive and a pharmaceutical cornucopia to keep you complacent."

His firm jaw softened and he blinked his eyes.

"What did they tell you about the woods yesterday? Because I can tell you right now, one of those stooges who came after you, Lewis or Granger, shot a dart in the side of your neck to take you down."

Asher clapped his hand against the left side of his neck. "They said I passed out."

"Yeah, like a lion passes out after a few hundred blow darts sink into him."

"I suspected something but didn't let on." He touched the back of his head. "I'm still pretty confused, but I pretended everything was great so that I'd have another opportunity to go outside…in case you came back."

"Well, I did." She reached for his thigh and stopped herself. He still thought of her as a stranger, but she planned to remedy that.

She grabbed the bottle of water in the cup holder instead. "Do you want some water?" She shook the bottle and the water sloshed back and forth. "It's not laced with anything—except my germs."

His hand hovered near the bottle for a couple of seconds and then he snatched it from her. He downed the rest of the water. "Sorry. Those damned drugs make me thirsty."

She looked away from the road and pointed to his feet. "We're going to have to take care of those."

"My feet are the least of my worries right now and I have plenty."

About a half hour later, they hit the outskirts of Mooseville and Paige tapped Asher's shoulder. "You should slump down in about five minutes, just until we get through the town. My motel is tucked away from the main drag. I can sneak you inside without a problem."

"I'm not going anywhere sitting in this car."

"Excuse me?" She always did have to deal with Asher's stubbornness, but his stubbornness combined with amnesia and fear just catapulted it to another dimension.

"It's too risky. Pull over now and I'll get in the trunk."

"The trunk?" Her gaze swept his large form, unchanged from weeks of captivity and bed rest.

"I can squeeze in. I'm not taking any chance of anyone seeing me in this town. Is it really called Mooseville?"

"It is and I will." She pulled over and popped the trunk from the inside of the car. They both got out and she lifted the lid of the trunk. "Make yourself comfortable."

"Looks like heaven compared to that hospital bed."

He crawled inside the trunk and his hospital gown spread open, revealing his mighty fine backside.

"Here, let's get you decent." She tugged the gown around his thighs, her fingers skimming his cold skin. She started to remove her jacket.

"Leave it on. You shouldn't look any different from when you left... Shut it."

Paige slammed the lid of the trunk on Asher, curled into a fetal position. She could do this, despite what her mother believed.

She drove through the sleepy town of Mooseville and pulled up to her room at the motel. She shouted over her shoulder. "I'm back at the motel. I'll just grab my stuff and check out."

After Asher gave his muffled assent, Paige slid from the car and pushed the door closed with a click. It took her ten minutes to throw her stuff in a bag. She dumped the three bottled waters from the fridge into a plastic bag, along with her leftover sandwich from the day before.

She strode to the motel office, swinging the room key from her finger. The bell on the door jingled when she swung it open.

Charlie, the motel's proprietor, peeked around the corner of the back office. His eyes widened when he saw her. "You'd better get out of here."

The key flew off her finger and her jaw dropped. "Why?"

"They're looking for you."

Goose bumps rippled across her flesh. "Who?"

"Those folks at the rest home on the hill." Charlie looked both ways as if the two of them weren't the only ones in the room. "Government folks."

She stooped to pick up the key and smacked it on the counter. "They're looking for me by name?"

"You...and others." He swept the key from the counter and dropped it in a drawer. "They came charging in here asking about this one and that one—

mostly men—but then they mentioned your name, Paige Sterling. Said you also might be using Paige Knight."

Paige gripped the strap of her purse. "They asked for me by name? What did they want to know?"

"If you'd been here, checked into the motel."

She glanced over her shoulder at the parking lot and her rental car with one big Delta Force soldier stashed in the trunk. "And you said…?"

Charlie folded his arms and narrowed his eyes. "Told 'em they'd need to come back with the cops and a search warrant if they wanted to see my guests' names. I did tell them I didn't have any single women staying here."

"Thank you, Charlie. I'm not involved in anything illegal."

He waved a hand. "I don't trust that bunch up there. Wouldn't give 'em the correct time of day if they asked."

"I don't trust them, either. I'm out of here. You can put the balance for the room on the credit card I used."

"Will do. Too bad I already ran it. That can be traced now."

"When I checked in here, I didn't realize…" She shook her head. "It's all right."

"Safe travels."

She slammed the office door harder than she'd intended and jogged to the car. She opened the back door and tossed her suitcase and pack onto the seat. When she slid behind the wheel, she turned her head to the side. "They're already looking for me, and others. They must realize you had help. The guy at the motel didn't tell them anything, so they can't know I'm the one who's here."

A thump resounded from the trunk, and Paige knew Asher had heard her.

She squealed out of the parking lot and raced toward the town. As she turned down the main street, she said, "Can you pound on the trunk again or something so I know you're still alive back there?"

Another loud thump answered her but did nothing to calm her nerves. "As soon as I get the chance, I'll let you out of there. We need a place to go."

She pulled up behind a white van at the one stoplight in town. The red light turned green, and she removed her foot from the brake pedal and held it above the accelerator as the car rolled forward.

The van hadn't moved, and she slammed on the brake. The car heaved forward and back. "Sorry, but there's some idiot who won't move."

Her hand slid from the steering wheel and rested on the horn in the center of it. "I'm going to give this guy two more seconds."

In less than a second, both doors of the van swung open and a hulking man dressed in the scrubs of a hospital orderly burst out of the passenger side and into the street.

He pinned her with a menacing glare and started to charge toward her.

"Oh my God, Asher. It's them. They found us."

Chapter Four

Adrenaline pumped through his body, and Asher's limbs jerked with the power of the sensation.

Paige screamed and he flushed with rage. She had to get out of here, had to move the car. Unless they had her boxed in. A car in front and one in back that she didn't notice?

He pounded on the roof of his prison with his fist. The car jumped in Reverse, and his head whacked the side of the trunk. He didn't even care. They were in motion.

He heard a man shouting. Sounded like that giant oaf Granger. The tires squealed and the smell of burning rubber assailed his nostrils.

The car jerked to the left. Asher felt like he was on some amusement park ride that kept you in the dark so you couldn't see the next turn of the track.

Paige must've floored it, because the car leaped forward and then the back fishtailed. As the car picked up speed, a crash echoed outside the trunk. Asher braced his body for an impact, wedging his bare feet against the side of the trunk…but none came.

The car hit a bump and then…nothing. It sailed forward. "Paige. Paige, can you hear me?"

Several seconds passed, and then he heard the sweetest sound ever.

"We're in the clear. The van that was blocking me crashed into another car."

Asher's lungs ached as he released a long breath in the close confines of the trunk. "Get as far away from here as possible and head south. Can you do that?"

Maybe Paige didn't have any breath left to answer, but as long as the car kept going forward he'd leave it in her capable hands.

Because his…fiancée had proved herself to be more than capable. In fact, she was a badass.

They traveled for what must've been at least thirty minutes before the car slowed down. It bumped and rumbled over rocky terrain before coming to a stop.

Paige threw open the trunk, and Asher blinked his eyes at the daylight.

"Are you okay?" They asked the question in unison, so he answered first.

"I'm fine. What the hell happened back there?" He uncurled his legs and swung one outside the trunk and then rolled out.

"Do you need to stretch out before getting into the passenger seat?"

"I just want out of this area." He picked his way to the front door of the car as pebbles and twigs attacked the soles of his feet.

Paige got behind the wheel and cranked up the heater. "You must be freezing."

"Hadn't noticed...until now." He rubbed his arms. "Are you going to tell me what went on with that van?"

She cranked her head over her shoulder and backed out of the outlet she'd pulled into. "Came up to the lone signal in Mooseville and pulled behind a white van. When the light changed, the van didn't move. I was about to pull around it when two goons in scrubs burst out of the van. I knew right away who they were. They must've been waiting for me—or any of your other friends on their list—to show up. They must've had my picture, and when they recognized me, they made their move."

"Now they know who helped me." And they knew that Paige was connected to him in some way. His fiancée. "How did you get away?"

"I reversed, and they jumped back into the van, but they weren't paying attention. The light had changed, and another car T-boned them." She smirked. "That van isn't going anywhere."

"Buys us some time."

She flicked her fingers at him. "We have to get you some clothes...and food. Are you hungry?"

"Not at all." He tapped on the window. "Not sure where we're going to buy clothes in the middle of nowhere."

"We're not exactly in the middle of nowhere. See those mountains?" She tipped her chin forward. "There's a ski resort up there, and it's open despite the lack of snow. They're manufacturing it now and expect the weather to cooperate in the next day or two for the Christmas holidays."

"You know this area?"

"No. Why would I know this area when I'm from Vegas?" She stopped and bit her bottom lip. "But you don't know that I'm from Vegas, do you?"

He reached out suddenly and touched her wrist. "No, but I'll remember. You'll tell me everything."

A smile wobbled on her lips. "Looking forward to it."

He pulled his hand back and dropped it in his lap as guilt nibbled at the edges of his mind. Touching her had been a calculated move on his part because he'd sensed her grief at his memory loss. His amnesia might even be worse for her. At least he didn't know what he was missing.

It had to be devastating to look into the eyes of someone who was supposed to love you and see a complete lack of recognition or feeling.

He stared out the window. Not a complete lack of feeling. Even locked in the trunk, he'd experienced an overpowering urge to protect this woman when she'd been in danger. Maybe that was normal under the circumstances, but he'd felt a tug at his heart when he first ran into her in the woods, too.

He'd get it all back. From what he'd seen of Paige so far, he had great taste in women.

"How much longer to the ski resort and do you think you can make it to a store before it closes and pick up some clothes for me?"

"Maybe an hour away. I know your sizes. Don't worry." A crease formed between her eyebrows. "Do you think it'll be safe? Would they have any reason to track us there?"

"Hell, I don't know. I don't even know why they'd *want* to track me down. What do they want with me?"

"I was hoping you could tell me. All I wanted to do was visit you, and the army officer who called me wouldn't tell me where you were. Didn't believe I was your fiancée."

"Why'd he call you?"

"I called the army trying to locate you when I heard about the incident. One of your team members called me to tell me about it, but he wouldn't tell me much. The army finally returned my call after they found my name and number in the favorites on your phone." She flexed her fingers on the steering wheel and then renewed her grip. "What happened, Asher? Do you remember?"

"That's what's weird." He scratched his jaw. "I do remember what happened right before my fall."

"That *is* unusual."

He jerked his head toward her. "You think so, too?"

"Since you don't know anything about me," she said with a sniff, "you don't know I'm a psychologist. I handle a lot of PTSD cases and repressed memories."

He raised his eyebrows. "That's convenient… A shrink. A shrinky-dinky."

She jerked the steering wheel. "Why did you say that?"

"Shrinky-dinky? I don't know. The silly phrase keeps coming to me every time I say or hear the word *shrink*." He studied her profile—the slightly upturned nose and the firm chin. "Why?"

"When I finished my hours and got licensed to practice, that's what you'd call me." She licked her lips. "You remembered that on your own."

"I did. Thank God. It's all going to come back, isn't it?"

She dropped her chin to her chest. "I can help you, Asher. I can help you recover your memories. It doesn't sound like the damage to your brain is permanent if a nickname came to you like that. Did the doctors mention anything about a permanent injury?"

"No. They kept assuring me that I'd fully recover my memory."

She let out a sigh. "That's good. It is strange though that you happen to remember the incident itself. What *did* happen? Can you tell me?"

"I can tell you. It's not classified or anything, and if it were, I guess I can't remember the classification level, anyway." He poked her in the side and got a smile out of her. "There are a few advantages to memory loss."

"There can be." Her pale cheeks flushed. "So, what happened out there in Afghanistan?"

"My commander, Major Rex Denver, was supposed to be having a meeting with a snitch from one of the groups that holds control of that area. The guy wanted to start feeding us intel and Denver was the man. He took me along and an army ranger. While we waited for the contact to show up, Denver took control. He shot the army ranger and then came at me. He took me off guard and pushed me off the edge of a cliff. I fell—" he tapped his head "—hit this thing and blacked out. An army ranger unit rescued me. Somehow, I managed to escape any severe physical injury, but I had a gash on the back of my head and I couldn't remember a damned thing when I came to."

"Except the incident that sent you over the edge."

"No."

"No?"

"I didn't remember that right away, either. That unfolded for me when I got to an army hospital in Germany and much more when they got me to Hidden Hills."

"Hidden Hills is an unfortunate name for that place." Paige lodged the tip of her tongue in the corner of her mouth. "That kind of selective memory is unusual."

"I stayed in Germany for a month before they shipped me to that crazy place. The hospital in Germany dealt more with my physical injuries—my head wound."

"And your Delta Force team members? Did they ever come to visit you?"

"No." Asher curled his hands into fists. "They didn't like what I had to say about Major Denver.

Didn't believe me and blamed me because Denver went AWOL."

"I tried calling a few of them, too, with no luck." Paige drummed her thumbs on the steering wheel. "Denver went AWOL after what happened with you?"

"Right after. Apparently, he took off after he attacked me. Left me for dead, but at least he got word to someone that my body was lying at the bottom of that drop-off."

"He did? He reported your location and condition?"

"Yeah, great guy, huh? He thought he'd killed me."

"D-do you remember Major Denver and the others?"

His eye twitched as pain throbbed against his temple. "No. I only recall Denver in that moment. I don't remember anything about him or working with him…or the others."

"Maybe it's your defense." She lifted her shoulders. "He did such a terrible thing to you, you've blocked out anything good about him to protect yourself."

"I don't know." He squeezed his eyes closed as the pain spread across his forehead.

"Grab my purse in the back seat." She jerked her thumb over her shoulder. "I have some ibuprofen in there. That plastic bag on the floor has some bottled water and a leftover sandwich if you're hungry."

He reached around and dragged her purse into the front seat. "Where?"

"The bottle's in the makeup bag."

He unzipped the little leopard-print bag and plucked a small bottle from it. He shook three gel caps into his hand and tossed them into his mouth. He chased them with a gulp of water and eased his head against the headrest. "I'm going to try to rest my eyes."

"Go ahead. I'll wake you up when we get there."

"I don't think I'll be falling asleep."

As much as he tried to keep his eyes open, closing them soothed the pain in his head and he allowed his heavy lids to drop. He would drift off, but something urgent kept prodding him and he'd jerk awake with a start.

In a short time he'd become dependent on the drugs that had eased his passage into sleep each night. He didn't want that anymore. He didn't claim to be any expert, like Paige apparently was, but being drugged up had to be interfering with his memories. How could he remember his past when half the time he couldn't remember what he'd eaten for lunch?

"Give in to it."

"What?" Opening one eye, he rolled his head to the side and pinned her with his gaze.

"You've been nodding off and jerking awake for the past forty-five minutes. Is it that you can't fall asleep or don't want to?"

"Maybe a little of both. Maybe I snore and drool in my sleep."

"You don't drool—at least not when you're sleeping."

He twisted his lips into a smile. This woman who knew him…intimately could do more to restore his memory than all the drugs and doctors in the entire US military.

Why had they tried to keep her away from him?

The signs that flew by the car window announced cabins and lift tickets and ski rentals. "We must be close."

"We are." She snatched her phone from the cup holder and tossed it at him. "First things first. Can you look up a clothing store? Even if it's a ski shop, I'm sure it'll have pants and shirts, jackets and boots."

He tapped the phone's display and then shook it. "No internet connection yet. We may have to drive straight to the ski resort to get connectivity. I'm sure there are stores there. Any reason you don't want to shop at the resort?"

"Those people from the prison…I mean rest home, might see this as a logical place for us to land."

"Probably, but we have a head start on them, and how do they know you didn't have clothing and an escape plan waiting for me?"

"I should have." She skimmed her hand along the side of her head. "When I saw the situation yesterday, I should've put more thought into breaking you out of there."

"I'd say you did a pretty good job." He plucked at

the hospital gown barely covering his thighs. "You didn't know they'd have me stripped and defenseless."

She snorted. "If they thought taking your clothing was enough to render you defenseless, they don't know Asher Knight like I know Asher Knight."

Tilting his head back and forth, he loosened the knots in his neck for probably the first time since he'd regained consciousness. Somebody knew him, and that deep pit of abandonment in his gut ached a little less.

He heaved out a sigh.

"Underwear, T-shirt, socks, jeans, long-sleeved shirt, boots and a jacket. Do I need to write that down?"

"You're the one with the memory problems, not me." She poked him in the side and grinned. "Like I said, I even know all your sizes. You stay slumped down in the seat while I go inside. I'm going to have to use my credit card though. I want to save the cash I have for later. Do you think the army is going to track me down through my credit card?"

He pointed out the window to the turnoff for the resort. "Very real possibility, but there's not much we can do about it. I have no money. No cash. No cards. No memory. No life."

She veered right onto the ramp and swiveled her head in his direction. "That escalated quickly. Are you okay? I mean other than the obvious?"

"Just a little brush with self-pity." He smacked the side of his face with his palm. "I've recovered now."

"You've shown zero self-pity. I think you're allowed a second or two."

"We need to come up with a way to get our hands on some cash. Maybe my old man stashed some away for a rainy day."

"Actually—" she slid him a sideways glance "—the feds thought he had, but he never copped to it."

"If he ever told me about it, I would've forgotten that along with everything else." He rubbed the goose bumps on his arms. The temperature had been steadily dropping outside and the heater inside hadn't kept pace with it.

Paige cranked it up higher. "We're not going to wait to find piles of cash somewhere while you freeze to death with no clothes."

The car bounced as she drove into a large parking lot for the ski resort. "We'll get you dressed and then maybe just get out of here. You don't really think it's the US Army that's after you, do you?"

"At first I took everything the army told me at face value. In Germany, my physical wounds were treated and everything seemed okay, except for the fact that my Delta Force unit wanted nothing to do with me because of my allegations against Major Denver. It's when they started messing with my mind and then sent me to that so-called rehabilitation center that things started rubbing me the wrong way."

"Let's put that on hold for now." She hunched over the steering wheel and peered through the windshield. "I see a clothing store on the periphery of the shops. Start scrunching down or it's back in the trunk with you."

He pushed the seat all the way back and slid down. "Go for it. This hospital gown is getting old…and baby blue is not my color."

She swung into a parking space. "Look at you, making jokes. You must be on the mend—and you look good in any color…or nothing at all."

Before he could think of a comeback, she slammed her door and the car shook.

How were they going to go anywhere under the radar if the army really was tracking Paige through her credit card? He didn't even know if he had any money. Let alone how to access it. His doctors had told him he was from Las Vegas. He must've met Paige there. Had he known her for a long time?

Even if he had money, they were about as far from Vegas as they could get.

He closed his eyes, although his instincts told him to keep watch. The orderlies in the van couldn't have gotten out of that mess fast enough to determine he and Paige would head for this ski resort and then give chase.

They might've sent word back to Hidden Hills and sent someone else up here to look for them though. He and Paige had made it easy for them, but the doctors at Hidden Hills had made it hard for him. Where else was he supposed to get clothes?

One thing he did know was they couldn't use Paige's credit card to check into some lodge or hotel here. They'd be sitting ducks.

A shadow passed over the car, and Asher's eyelids flew open. He inched his head up and pinned his gaze to the rearview mirror. A figure moved behind the car.

Asher ducked his head, clenching his fists, holding them at the ready. They were the only weapons he had and wouldn't be very effective against a gun—not that his jailers at Hidden Hills could get away with murdering him in a parking lot. Could they?

In the silence of the car as he waited, his heart hammered in his ears. The rush of adrenaline ebbed and flowed in his body and he fought off the dizziness it caused.

If the guy had spotted him in the car, why hadn't he made a move? Asher scooted up in his seat and looked in the rearview mirror first. The man had moved on—probably just someone making his way through the parking lot.

Asher sat up straighter and his gaze swept the lot. A shuttle bus waited at the curb at the base of the broad steps that led to the shops and ultimately the ski lifts. A few people were milling around the steps. When the shuttle pulled away, two women and a solo man were left behind.

The women seemed to be conferring about something over their phones, but the man watched…and waited.

Asher kept his eye on him as the man's head swiveled from the parking lot to the shops. Was he waiting for his wife?

He could be the man who'd passed by Paige's car.

Asher didn't see any other single men in the parking lot and not another man in red plaid.

Asher locked on to him, studying his every move. When Paige appeared at the top of the steps laden down with shopping bags, Asher sat up, every sense on high alert.

The stranger seemed to come to attention, too. He turned his back to the parking lot to watch Paige's descent, his hands shoved in his jacket pockets.

With his fingertips buzzing, Asher clicked open the car door. His first step on the cold asphalt with his bare foot sent a shock through his system, but it only served to jolt him into action.

He left the car unlocked and then weaved through the parked vehicles, ducking and crouching in case the man decided to peel his eyes from Paige.

As she hit the last step, her vision and movement hampered by the bags swinging from her arms and clutched to her chest, the stranger made his move.

He reached his arm out to Paige as if in assistance…but Asher knew better. He shot forward, shouting and waving his arms.

"I'm here. I'm here. I'm the one you want."

Chapter Five

Paige had been moving away from the man and now she turned her face toward Asher barreling down on both of them. Her mouth dropped open and she stumbled to the side, away from the stranger and his outstretched hand, the rest of his body twisted in Asher's direction.

His right hand still out of his pocket, the man swiveled around to face Asher. He swayed to his left and in a split second Asher took advantage of his imbalance.

He charged the man, his hospital gown flapping around him, and shouted. "Run, Paige!"

With a few feet between him and the stranger, Asher made a flying tackle at him that would've made his friend Cam the football player proud. Before the man could reach into his pocket for whatever weapon he had, Asher drove his shoulder into the guy's chest, knocking him backward onto the steps.

The two women several feet away screamed.

The man's hand clawed at his pocket, but Asher pinned the hand with his knee, driving it into the cold cement. He grunted, and Asher gave him more to grunt about as he smashed his fist against the man's nose. Blood spouted and Asher followed up with a punch to the gut.

A woman was screeching behind him. "We're calling the police."

Asher landed another punch to the side of the man's head. As he drew back his fist for another onslaught, a car horn blared behind him.

He twisted his head over his shoulder, and Paige's rental car squealed to a halt at the shuttle stop. His hand jerked to a stop in midair, and he plunged it into the man's pocket. His fingers curled around a syringe.

He pulled it out as Paige honked again. The man groaned beneath him and Asher jabbed him in the side of the neck with the needle.

A few more people had gathered at the top of the steps and Asher knew the cops wouldn't be far behind. He pulled the needle from the man's neck, staggered to his feet and jumped into Paige's car, which she'd already put into motion.

She floored it out of the parking lot, and the car bounced like it was in a movie chase scene when she rolled off the curb into the street.

"Oh my God. You're bleeding."

"I think that's his blood."

"No." She reached over and rubbed his burning knuckles. "Your hand is bleeding."

"That's from hitting him. I took him by surprise

and he didn't get many shots in." He held up the needle. "He was counting on using this."

Paige gasped. "Throw it out the window."

"So somebody else, maybe a kid, could pick it up?" He dropped it on the floor of the back seat. "I'll wrap it up and dispose of it later."

"I screwed up. We shouldn't have come here." She slammed the heel of her hand against the steering wheel. "Of course this would be the first place they'd look."

"We had to come here. We didn't have a choice."

She pressed her fingers against her cheek. "And your poor feet, running around out there in the cold, fighting in a hospital gown."

"Don't worry about me. I should've never sent you out there on your own. I should've realized someone would be staking out the ski resort."

She lifted her eyebrows. "You couldn't exactly go shopping in that getup."

"I need to get out of this." He plucked at the hospital gown. "I need to start feeling human…and then there's going to be hell to pay."

PAIGE GLANCED AT him as she smoothed her hands over the steering wheel. They'd finally stopped shaking, but Asher's words sent a new jolt of adrenaline through her system.

"What do you mean?"

"I'm going to figure out who's doing this to me and why, and I'm not going to stop until I have all the answers…and all my memories."

"Where can we go now?" She adjusted the rearview mirror and released a small breath.

"There's no real snow yet, right? There must be hundreds of cabins in this area, vacant for at least a few more weeks until the holidays."

She swallowed. "You're suggesting we break into someone's empty cabin and make ourselves at home?"

"Just until we can get our bearings, and I can put some clothes on." He jerked his finger over his shoulder. "Whoever that guy was back there, he's out. His associates are going to figure we've fled the area."

"We should flee the area."

"Let's do the unexpected." He tapped on the window. "Make the next turn."

For the next twenty minutes, Asher guided her through mountain roads and turnouts like he knew the place. After surveying and abandoning several prospective cabins, he had her follow a road into a heavily wooded area where a single cabin nestled against the side of a mountain.

"This one."

"How do you know someone's not living here?"

"Do you see any vehicles? Any pets? Any life at all?"

Her eyes darted around the property. "No, but it doesn't mean there won't be."

"We'll play it by ear."

She jabbed his thigh with her finger. "I think you forgot how cautious you used to be."

"I was Delta Force. I couldn't have been that cautious."

"You *are* Delta Force, and I guess *cautious* is the wrong word. Maybe I mean organized. You like to plan."

"This *is* a plan. It's the only viable one right now except to go on the run."

"In a hospital gown."

"Right. Park in the back."

She swung the car to the right on the dirt road that curved around the house and continued through the trees in the back. Luckily the snow had held off so far this season, or it would've piled up in front of them. Now they just rolled over cold, frozen ground.

Ducking her head, she peered through the windshield. "Do you think they have security cameras?"

"If they do, I'll have to disable them."

As Paige stepped out of the car, her shoe crunched the gravel and the sound seemed to echo in the woods. She tipped her head back and scanned the edges of the roof for security equipment.

Asher appeared next to her. "I don't see anything, do you?"

"No." She pointed to his feet. "You could've at least put on the boots I bought for you."

He curled his toes into the gravel. "I'm getting kind of used to being barefoot."

"I'll get them." She buried her head in the back seat of the car, where she'd tossed the bags in her mad rush to get back to Asher fighting with the stranger. She backed out of the car with the bags hanging from her arms and turned to face the cabin, leaving her own suitcase and laptop on the seat.

Asher waved from the cement slab behind the cabin. "I think I found a way in."

She strode toward him, the bags banging against her thighs. "I feel like a thief."

"We're not going to steal anything...except some soap and water." He rubbed his hands together. "And maybe some firewood."

A few minutes later, Asher had jimmied the lock on the back door. He rested his hand on the door-knob. "Are you ready?"

"For flashing lights and guard dogs?"

"Something like that." He eased open the door.

Paige held her breath, but nothing came at them. A hushed silence even emanated from the woods behind the cabin. Would they finally get a moment's peace? She had so much to tell Asher.

He widened the door, and they faced a mudroom, four pairs of ski boots lined up against one wall.

Paige nudged the toe of one of the boots. "Doesn't look like they've been worn recently."

Asher snapped the door closed behind them and locked the top dead bolt. "I think we're safe...for now."

"That'll be a first since you arrived in Vermont."

"I think that'll be a first since I left on that assignment with Major Denver."

Asher led the way into the kitchen, clear of clutter and dishes, waiting for its inhabitants to bring it to life.

Paige grabbed the handle of the fridge and yanked open the door. Empty shelves greeted her.

"They clean out at the end of the season." She plucked a bottle of ketchup from inside the refrigerator door. "Unless you feel like some ketchup."

"I'm guessing they turn off the gas." Asher cranked a knob on the stove. "Yeah, that's going to be one cold shower."

"There is a potbellied stove with a little wood stacked up next to it."

"Are you planning to heat up buckets of water and pour them in the tub for me like a pioneer woman?" He dropped the bags at his feet.

"No, but you can warm up once you get out of your cold shower and get dressed."

"I think I'll skip the full shower and just wash up in the sink."

"Just get out of that hospital gown." She felt the heat wash into her cheeks. "And get into those clothes."

He tilted his head. "I know it's an awkward situation between us, but you don't have to blush like a schoolgirl and clarify every double entendre."

"You're right. It's awkward and I'm awkward, so I'm going to cover by looking for some first-aid supplies. You could use some antiseptic on those feet."

"Let me get that fire started first."

"Go." She flattened her hands against his broad back and gave him a small shove. "Clean up and get dressed. I'll worry about the fire. I was a Girl Scout, remember?"

He lifted one eyebrow. "If you say so."

She smacked her hand against her forehead. "I am so sorry. It's just…"

"Don't worry about it." He encircled her wrists with his fingers. "You don't have to watch what you say around me. Treat me like a normal person, and I might just start feeling like one."

Even this light touch from him felt like coming home, and her body ached to fall against him and have him take care of everything like he always did. She shook her head. They were way beyond that.

It was her turn to take care of him now, get him back on track. She could do it.

He released her wrists as quickly as he'd claimed them. "I'm going to leave the fire in your capable hands, Girl Scout."

"There must be a full bathroom upstairs in the loft." She jerked open a door below the stairs. "This one's just a half bath."

"Maybe that's all I need." He hunched his shoulders in the thin material of the hospital gown. "I'm not going to soak in a cold tub."

"No, but you need to dip those feet into some water—cold or not."

"Yes, ma'am." He saluted and took the stairs two at a time while clutching the robe behind him with one hand and holding the shopping bags in the other.

Paige crouched before the potbellied stove and wadded up some newspaper from the stack next to the woodpile. She glanced at the date before crumpling the next one in her fist and mumbled, "Last year. Place has probably been empty for that long."

She shoved pieces of wood into the stove on top of her kindling and lit the corner of a paper with a long match. She touched the match around the edges of her pile and sat back on her haunches as the flames lapped toward the wood.

With the fire crackling in the stove and the water running intermittently upstairs, Paige searched a closet under the stairs. She pulled out a blanket and tucked it under her arm. Standing on her tiptoes, she felt the top shelf for a first-aid kit but came up empty.

Hugging the blanket to her chest, she raised her gaze to the loft. Maybe there were some medical supplies in the bathroom upstairs.

She was engaged to Asher, had lived with him and would've thought nothing of barging into the bathroom with him in it. And if he were in the shower, nine times out of ten he would've pulled her in with him.

Her nose tingled, and she swiped her hand across it. She'd have to take it slowly. Asher didn't know her from one of the crazy nurses at Hidden Hills. She'd have to gain his trust and had already come a long way in that direction after the events of today. She'd also have to use her professional skills on him to help him recover his memories. It wasn't just their love that depended on it now—it was Asher's life.

She shook out the blanket and placed it on a rug

in front of the stove, now cranking out heat like a little ball of burning lava.

"Feels warmer already."

She tipped her head back to see Asher leaning over the wood railing that bordered the loft, dressed in jeans and a green flannel shirt that matched his eyes. She'd recognized the color immediately in the store.

"Could you look for some bandages and ointments in the bathroom?"

He held up a square red bag and dangled it in the space above her. "Already found it."

"Come on down, then. It's getting cozy." Did that sound like a come-on? "I mean it's warm down here. B-by the stove."

She'd just shut up now.

"On my way."

He jogged down the stairs with more energy than he had a right to have. He hit the bottom step and tossed the red bag to her. "That water was cold, but it felt good."

"Seems like it energized you. Maybe you should roll around in the snow." She waved her hand at the window.

"It's snowing?" His stride ate up the distance between the stairs and the front window and he flicked back the drapes with one finger.

"I mean if it were. Looks like it's coming soon."

"Whew." He stepped back. "We don't need snow right now bringing people back to this cabin."

She unzipped the first-aid kit. "How are your feet? Let me take a look."

"Not bad, considering what I put them through."

She sank to the floor in front of the stove and patted the seat of the chair she'd drawn up to the heat. "Sit."

He folded his large frame into the chair and stretched out his legs. "The clothes are a good fit. Waist is a little big on the jeans, but nothing a belt won't fix."

"I didn't get you a belt." She took his right foot and propped it on her knee. "You probably lost a little weight while in…captivity."

He whistled. "That's exactly what it was."

"You have a few slivers on the soles of your feet." She reached behind her for her purse, dragged out her makeup bag and poked around for her tweezers. "Aha."

Pinching them together, she held them up. "These should do the trick."

She traced the bottom of his foot, the skin soft from the soap and water, and located the three slivers lodged into the epidermis. She swiped an antiseptic wipe across the tips of the tweezers and aimed for the first sliver. When she'd pulled out the third one, she tapped his other foot. "Let me get this one while I have the tools ready."

He switched feet. "Don't tickle me again. I'm very ticklish."

She whispered, "I know."

She plucked out just one sliver from his other foot.

She then dabbed all the raw spots on his feet with another antiseptic wipe. "I don't think anything needs bandaging."

"I hope not. I wouldn't be able to walk much less run with my feet bandaged."

"You planning to do a lot of running?" She peered at him over his toes.

"Oh, yeah. Until I can figure out what the hell is going on with my life."

"I can help with that, too." She tapped the side of her head. "I'm going to start by hypnotizing you, Asher."

"Let's do it." He pulled his legs back beneath him, and hunched forward, arms crossed on his knees.

"I don't work on an empty stomach. I don't know about you, but I need to eat something first. It's past dinnertime."

"Did you see anything besides ketchup in that kitchen?"

"I didn't look in the cupboards, but I picked up some trail mix, nuts and beef jerky in the store when I was shopping for your clothes."

He snorted. "Do I look like a squirrel?"

"Would you be happier with cold beans from a can, or whatever they might have in the cupboards?"

"Actually, beef jerky sounds pretty good right now."

She hopped to her feet, her proximity to Asher making it hard to concentrate on food or anything else. She grabbed one of the plastic bags and dug through it. "It's actually turkey jerky. Is that okay?"

"Bring it on."

She tossed him the bag of jerky on her way to the kitchen. "I'm going to wash my hands. Do you need anything?"

"Water." The plastic crackled as he ripped into the jerky bag. "Do you think you can do it?"

"What? Get you water?" She cranked on the faucet and opened a cupboard to look for a cup.

"Hypnotize me."

She let his words hang in the air as she filled a glass with tap water. She approached him with the water in one hand and a bag of trail mix in the other. She dangled the trail mix in front of him, but he shook his head.

"You're susceptible to hypnosis. I can do it."

He ripped off a piece of jerky with his teeth and chewed for several seconds. "Can I tell you what I want to remember first, or is it just a free-for-all of memories?"

Shaking open the bag of trail mix, she scoped out all the cashews and took her time answering. "I can pinpoint memories through suggestion. What do you want to remember first?"

He dropped the jerky and wiped his fingers together. "I want to know what happened on that ridge in Afghanistan."

His answer pierced a little hole in her heart. He didn't even know about Ivy.

"I'm sorry."

"N-no. I understand. That was the moment you lost your memory. Why not start there?"

"I think understanding what happened at that moment is imperative right now. Knowing what occurred will keep us safe. Maybe it holds the clue as to why I was locked up at Hidden Hills."

"Of course." She plucked out a few more cashews and glanced up. "What?"

"When do we get started?"

"You didn't finish your—" she waved her hand in his direction "—dinner."

"I'd rather start working on regaining my memories… All of them eventually."

Her heart fluttered. She should just tell him about Ivy. She didn't have to wait until he remembered his own daughter. Of course, if she told him they had a four-year-old together, he'd wonder why they hadn't gotten married yet.

Then she'd have to tell him all that other stuff.

He clasped his hands and pinned them between his knees. "The sooner the better."

She knew Asher had a stronger desire right now to find out what happened on that mission with Major Denver than to learn about his life with her, and as much as she wanted to tell him all about their romance and their beautiful daughter, she wasn't in any hurry to divulge the rocky road their relationship had taken. Now she had an excuse to keep it hidden a bit longer.

"That's not going to happen with you sitting all hunched over like that." She licked some salt from her fingertips. "I'm going to wash my hands and find an object of concentration to use. You sit back in that chair and relax."

She rose from where she'd parked herself on the arm of the sofa across from Asher and peered out the front window.

Asher shifted in the chair, twisting his head over his shoulder. "See anything?"

"No, and no snow yet, either." She twitched the curtain back into place. "I think we're still safe."

"Even if they think we stayed in the area, they have a lot of cabins to search. Doesn't mean they won't find this one though."

She turned from the window and flicked the back of his head with her finger, avoiding his neat scar. "You're supposed to be relaxing, not thinking about the next attack."

"Attack—that's what's going on, isn't it? Hidden Hills wants me back."

"And maybe we can find out why." She jerked open a drawer and the stainless-steel utensils inside rattled. "This should do it."

Asher's eyes widened when she walked toward him with a knife. "Is that supposed to help me relax?"

"Exactly. You need something to watch, something to focus on."

"You mean like a swinging pendant, Shrinky-dinky?"

She pointed the blade of the knife at him. "You can wipe the smirk off your face. That's how it works."

Stretching his arms in front of him, he rolled his shoulders. "I'm ready."

"Okay. It shouldn't be too hard for you to clear your mind, so breathe deeply and think of something pleasant." She pulled her chair forward and sank into the soft cushion, her knees almost bumping Asher's.

Too bad that something pleasant wouldn't be her.

"Breaking out of Hidden Hills was about as pleasant as it gets." He blinked. "Should I close my eyes or leave them open?"

"Open." She held up the knife. "Watch the shiny object for a while first, listen to my voice, keep breathing. If you begin to feel like you want to close your eyes, do so."

He leaned back, the muscles in his face relaxing, and she realized how taut he'd been holding himself. He must be in a world of hurt and confusion right now. She couldn't even imagine being in the limbo he must be experiencing.

"Watch this." She held up the knife, and it caught the flickering light of the fire, which made the knife look like a wand glinting with magic. She hoped it could work some magic tonight.

"I'm watching."

"Listen to my voice, and pay attention to your breathing—in and out. Make sure your breathing is consistent."

For several minutes, Paige led him into a deep state of subconsciousness and then snapped her fingers.

His head lifted, his eyes still closed.

"You can open your eyes, if you like. I'm going to take you back to that mission in Afghanistan with Major Denver. Who else was with you?"

Asher's mouth opened and then closed.

"It's okay. You can talk, answer my questions."

"Army ranger. We were with an army ranger named Dylan Curran."

"What was the mission? What were you doing there?"

"It was secret."

"You can tell me." She touched his knee.

"Major Denver was meeting with an insurgent, someone playing both sides. He had information for Denver, important information."

"Did you ever meet this insurgent?"

"We were waiting for him."

"While you were waiting for him, Major Denver shot the ranger?"

"No." Asher's chin dropped to his chest.

"Don't fall asleep. If Major Denver didn't shoot the ranger, what happened to Dylan?"

"He was shot."

A frisson of fear whispered across the back of her neck. "Who shot him? D-did you shoot Dylan?"

"No."

She released a small breath between puckered lips. "So, Major Denver shot Dylan and then he pushed you off the cliff?"

"No. No. Stop." Asher's body stiffened, and his face contorted. "Shots fired. Stop. Take cover. Stop."

"It's okay, Asher. You're not on the cliff anymore. I'm bringing you out now." She snapped her fingers.

His shoulders dropped, and his chest rose and fell rapidly.

The hypnotic state should've relaxed him, but he'd become agitated as she took him back to that place. It was best to bring him out, even if he didn't get as far as they'd wanted.

She squeezed his thigh. "Are you okay?"

His eyelids flew open and he pinned her with a burning gaze. "I remember. I remember what happened."

"You do? That's great. A great first step." Now maybe she could get him to remember her and their daughter.

"Great? I don't think so."

"Why?" That fear crept back across her flesh.

"They lied to me, Paige. Major Denver never shot that army ranger. Never pushed me off the cliff. It was all a setup…and they used me and my amnesia to perpetrate it."

Chapter Six

Asher shook his head, trying to escape the fog from the hypnosis.

Paige snapped her fingers again, and the crack penetrated his brain like a bolt of lightning.

"You're awake now." She spoke the words as a command, not a question, and it dragged him all the way back to consciousness.

She handed him his glass of water. "Why would those doctors at Hidden Hills implant false memories in your brain? Memories that would implicate Major Denver?"

"I have no idea, but that's exactly what they did. Right? They must've put those scenes in my head." He dug his fingers into the indentations of both temples. "They're obviously after me, after us now, because they don't want me to remember the truth."

"When you were under, you stopped answering my questions and I brought you out of your hypnotic state because you were getting agitated. You must've been going through the scene on your own. If it wasn't Denver, do you remember who *did* shoot the ranger and attack you? Was it the insurgent you were supposed to meet?"

"I don't know. We never saw Denver's contact. He never showed up."

"Did you see who shot Dylan?"

"No. I heard the shot and Dylan dropped. Denver and I looked at each other, and the shooter took a shot at me and missed. Denver *did* push me, but he was pushing me behind a boulder. Nobody pushed me off that cliff. I slipped when I was trying to avoid the bullets raining down on us."

"*Could* it have been the guy you were supposed to be meeting, shooting at you from a distance? Maybe he and Denver arranged for him to kill you and Dylan. Maybe that's what the army doctors were driving at."

"He saved my life, Paige. Major Denver saved my life, and there's no way he'd kill a ranger." He drove his fist into his thigh. "How could I ever have believed that?"

"When you woke up, you didn't know Major Denver from Colonel Sanders. You wouldn't have remembered his character or anything else about him."

Clasping his hands behind his neck, Asher asked, "What the hell is going on? Why would anyone try to set up Denver? And if I hadn't rolled off the side of that cliff and injured my head, would I be dead right now?"

Paige lifted her shoulders, about the only answer he could expect to his rhetorical question.

"I need to find out who was behind setting up

Denver, setting me up. Did they really think they could get away with implanting those false memories in my head?"

"In a way I'm glad they did."

"Why?" He sat up in the chair and studied her face, a face too beautiful to ever forget.

"Think about it. Whoever shot that army ranger and shot at you didn't plan on leaving any witnesses. The people behind this setup must've panicked when they realized you survived that fall—until they found out you had no memory of the events." She leveled a finger at him. "Your amnesia saved your life."

Paige was happy he had amnesia, even though he couldn't remember her, remember their life together?

"Saved my life and strengthened their narrative. Who better to implicate Major Rex Denver in a traitorous plot than one of his own loyal Delta Force men?"

"And now they've lost you." She twisted her fingers together. "They're never going to allow you to tell the real story. They'll do everything in their power to discredit you."

"You and I both know they're going to do more than discredit me." Asher pinched the bridge of his nose and squeezed his eyes shut. "They want me back."

"They, they, they. Who is they?"

"If I knew that, I'd be halfway to recovery. When people in the government, the army, people you're supposed to be able to trust, turn on you, anyone can be the enemy."

"Anyone but me." She dropped to her knees in front of his chair and took his hands in hers. "I hope you know that, even if you don't remember me."

"I know that. You've proved yourself over and over today." He squeezed her fingers. "Should we get going on those memories now?"

"You mean through hypnosis?" She shook her head from side to side. "Not tonight. You've had enough."

"Why don't you just tell me, then? Tell me a story about how a fearless psychologist wound up with a messed-up Delta Force soldier."

"Fearless? Messed up? I think you have us confused." She tipped her head back and laughed at the ceiling. "You were far from messed up, Asher."

"I do know my father is in prison for bank robbery. My mother is dead. Doesn't exactly sound like a prescription for sound mental health."

"You fought through it."

His brows shot up. "Were you my therapist?"

"No. That would've been unethical." She released his hands and crossed her legs beneath her. "We met at a party. You came with a buddy who was friends with my friend's cousin."

He rolled his eyes. "I'm going to need hypnosis again just to straighten that out."

"It was a birthday party at one of the hotels on the Strip. It got kinda crazy and you saved me."

"I did?" He hunched forward, burying his chin in his palm as if listening to a story about two strangers…which he was. "Tell me more."

"The party was out by the pool and…some drunken idiot got the bright idea to take the party *into* the pool. People started jumping in, with and without their clothes, and someone pushed me in, fully clothed, holding a drink. My arm hit the side of the pool and my glass broke, cutting my hand. You jumped in and rescued me."

"I was watching you from across the deck."

"You remember?" Her cheeks flushed and her blue eyes brightened.

He didn't want to disappoint her, but he didn't want to lie, either. "No. I'm just embellishing the story. I saw a pretty blonde across the pool deck, kept my eye on her, and when I saw her flailing in the water, I did my Delta Force thing and jumped in. I must've thought it was a stroke of good luck that she needed my help."

She tilted her head to one side. "I don't believe you're that conniving."

He wiggled his eyebrows up and down. "Maybe I am."

"You just like saving people." She hit his knee-cap with her fist.

"You do, too."

"Me?"

"You're a therapist. You help people every day." He tapped the side of his head. "You just helped me. Why do you work with people who have PTSD?"

She drew her knees to her chest and wrapped her arms around her legs. "My dad was a cop. He suffered from PTSD and wound up…dead."

Sympathy flared in his chest, and he put his hand over his heart. "I'm sorry. Seems crazy the daughter of a cop would want to go out with the son of a criminal."

"You're not your father." She wrinkled her nose. "And I'm not mine."

"Why wouldn't you want to be like him? Cops are heroes, straight up, every day."

Paige sucked her bottom lip between her teeth. "My dad committed suicide."

His stomach dropped. How much pain could this woman endure? And he was just adding to it.

He slid off the chair and crouched in front of her on the floor. "I'm sorry, and here I am making you go through all this again."

She met his gaze with her blue eyes that held all the keys to his life.

"You know what? You responded to this news with all the same sincerity and compassion you're showing now. That's when I knew I wanted you forever, and nothing's changed...for me."

He drew one finger along her smooth cheek and touched her trembling bottom lip. "Nothing's going to change for me, either, Paige. What you've done for me already, getting me out of Hidden Hills, is enough to show me what you're made of, what we had together. And we'll have it again."

Her lashes fluttered, and her lips parted in invitation.

He wanted to kiss her, but it felt false. Did he have

a right to kiss her? Leaning in, he closed his eyes and stopped analyzing.

Brushing her lips with his sent an electric current charging through his body. That had to mean something. He rested his forehead against hers to steady himself, and her warm breath bathed his cheek.

She turned her head and whispered against his ear. "I do have something to tell you about us, something you need to know."

His muscles tensed as he prepared for another betrayal. Had this all been some kind of setup?

He jerked away from her and held up one hand.

"Y-you don't want to hear it yet?"

"I want to hear everything you have to say, Paige, but I think there's someone outside the cabin."

She scrambled to her feet, bumping his chin with her head. "It's either the owners or someone tracked us down. What did you hear?"

He pushed up from the floor. "The engine of a car—too close for a vehicle passing on the mountain road."

Hunching forward, he crept to the front window, lifted one corner of the curtains and peered into the black night. "I don't see anything, no lights, although they wouldn't come driving to the front door."

"They would if they were the owners of the cabin." Paige had come up behind him and stuck her fingers into his pocket.

"Around the back, then. There's another road to this cabin through the woods." He shifted away from the window and headed to the mudroom that led to the back door of the cabin. He pressed his ear against the door, his hand on the doorknob.

"Anything?" Paige hovered at his shoulder.

"You stay here. Scream if someone tries to come through the back. I'm going around to try to surprise him."

"I'll do more than scream." She picked up a ski pole and thrust it in front of her. "Anyone coming through that door is going to get the sharp end of this."

"Be careful." He squeezed her arm on his way out of the mudroom.

He grabbed his new jacket, went to the front door and eased it open. He scanned the empty gravel drive in front of the cabin before stepping out onto the porch.

He sniffed the air like a wolf on the hunt and then slipped around the side of the house. When he rounded the corner, he stumbled to a stop and braced his hand against the side of the cabin.

A figure dressed all in black hunched over the driver's side of Paige's rental car, and another car was parked behind it—it must have come from the woods.

An energy force slammed against his chest and he launched himself at the stranger. The man squeaked as Asher crushed him against the car.

Asher grabbed the intruder by the back of the neck and swung his body around, lifted him off his feet before slamming him to the ground.

The man groaned and rolled over.

Asher stomped on his flailing wrist in case he had a weapon nearby, although Asher didn't see any weapons.

Paige materialized beside him, panting and brandishing the ski pole. "I saw the other car from the window in the back, and then I saw him lurking around my car. Who is he?"

His galloping heart slowing to a trot, Asher leaned over the figure writhing on the ground and ripped the ski mask from his face.

Paige gasped. "What the hell?"

The woman on the ground choked out, "Please, Asher. I want to help. I—I love you."

Chapter Seven

Paige jerked her head toward Asher, his foot still firmly planted on the woman's wrist. "Do you know her? Who is this?"

"A nurse from Hidden Hills—Tabitha Crane." Asher bent over and hauled Tabitha to her feet. He spun her around and shoved her against the car. "Any weapons?"

He patted her down in a way she must've relished if she really did love Asher. He hadn't touched Paige that intimately yet.

The woman sucked in a breath, obviously still hurting from the rough treatment. "I don't have any weapons."

Asher yanked Tabitha against his chest, his arm around her neck. "Anyone with you?"

"I'm alone. I swear, Asher. There's nobody else."

Her voice hitched on a sob, and Paige caught the double meaning of her words, even if Asher didn't.

He released her and shoved her toward the open door to the mudroom. "Get inside. You have some questions to answer."

Tabitha moved slowly, her right arm dangling beside her. She tripped over the door's threshold and Paige instinctively caught her arm to steady her.

That earned Paige a scowl from Asher, and she shrugged. If they wanted to question Tabitha, they couldn't allow her to collapse.

When they got to the living room with the heat emanating from the potbellied stove and the wrappers from their makeshift dinner littering the coffee table, Tabitha's eyes widened. "What is this place?"

Asher shoved her into the chair he'd vacated earlier and growled, "We're asking the questions."

"Do you want some water?" Paige tapped her own chin where Tabitha's had an abrasion.

"Yes, please. Who are you?"

Asher stepped between them and pointed a finger at Tabitha. "Be quiet, and the water can wait until she's answered a few questions."

Paige knew all about Asher's no-nonsense approach. She'd been the recipient of it and she didn't kid herself about what he did as a D-Boy, but his tone with Tabitha still made her flinch.

Paige pulled up the other chair close to the stove and rubbed her hands together. "We want her to be able to answer questions."

"Oh, she'll answer our questions." He loomed over Tabitha and crossed his arms. "How did you track us here?"

Tabitha's head swiveled. "Where's the hospital gown?"

Asher took a deep breath, his chest expanding,

which made him look even more imposing. "What does that matter?"

"That's how I tracked you." Tabitha blinked her eyes, her light-colored lashes giving her a surprised look.

But Asher seemed like the surprised one. "What do you mean? How did the hospital gown lead you to me?"

"Go get it, and I'll show you."

Afraid Asher would rebuff Tabitha again, Paige bounded from her chair. "I'll get it. It's upstairs in the bathroom."

She rushed up the staircase to the bathroom and scooped up the hospital gown Asher had dropped in the corner. For a few seconds, Paige pressed it against her face to inhale his scent.

She dangled the gown in front of her as she scurried back down to the interrogation. "Here it is."

"Check the hem." Tabitha tipped her head toward Paige and winced, grabbing the back of her neck.

Paige felt along the hem of the gown and felt something hard sewn into the material. "What is it?"

"It's a GPS tracker."

Asher lunged for the gown and snatched it out of Paige's hand. With his bare hands, he ripped the material apart and pinched a small, black device between his fingers. "Is this still active?"

"It is." Tabitha held up her hands. "But I'm the only one who can track it, nobody else."

"You put a GPS tracker on me?" Asher spit out

the words and then tossed the device into the fire, where it popped and sizzled.

Tabitha ran her hands through her stringy hair. "Better that than injected in your body."

Asher narrowed his eyes. "What do you mean?"

"The doctors had orders to inject a tracker under your skin after the incident in the forest." She pulled back her shoulders and folded her hands in her lap. "I convinced them you'd notice, as you'd already recovered from your physical injuries. I suggested the GPS be sewn into the hem of a hospital gown and that we keep you in it."

"Had orders?"

Asher had latched on to the same words that had jumped out at Paige—well, that and the fact Tabitha seemed quite pleased to keep Asher in a hospital gown under her watchful eye.

Spreading her hands, Tabitha said, "Don't ask me whose orders. I don't know."

Paige cleared her throat. "Tell us about the facility. Hidden Hills is supposed to be a rehab center for injured soldiers, right?"

"Yes, but not physical injuries. There is some of that, but we handle soldiers suffering from PTSD and other psychological traumas."

"Are they all prisoners, like Asher?"

A flush crawled from Tabitha's neck into her face. "Prisoners? Asher wasn't a prisoner. Who are you again?"

"Not a prisoner?" Asher snorted. "GPS trackers,

drugging, implanted memories. If those things don't scream imprisonment, I don't know what does."

"Implanted memories?" Tabitha's eye twitched and Paige almost believed her.

Asher uncrossed his arms and rolled his shoulders. "Okay, we'll play it your way—for now. What did the doctors tell you about me?"

Tabitha's tongue darted from her mouth as her gaze shifted from Asher to Paige and back again. "They told me you might be involved in traitorous activity involving Major Rex Denver and an insurgent he was meeting. They thought you might be lying about your amnesia to avoid answering questions."

"Damn them." Asher smacked a fist into his palm. "Instead of implanting memories to implicate myself, they manufactured a remembrance that would crush Denver. But why?"

Paige smoothed her hand down Asher's corded forearm where his veins popped out from his flesh. She turned toward Tabitha, who had her gaze pinned to Paige's hand.

Paige snatched her hand back. Maybe they should allow Tabitha to believe she had a chance with Asher to get more info out of her. The woman couldn't really believe Asher felt anything but contempt for her, could she?

She studied Tabitha's light-colored eyes, gleaming with light as they rested on Asher, and felt a stab of pity. Tabitha adored her fiancé, and it didn't resemble a normal attraction. They'd have to watch this woman. She might even be lying to them right now.

There was one sure way of finding out. Paige tucked her hand through Asher's arm and snuggled in closer to him, watching Tabitha's face blanch.

Paige cleared her throat. "What did you hear about Major Denver at Hidden Hills?"

"What?" Tabitha dragged her gaze away from Paige's contact with Asher, who hadn't moved a muscle.

"Major Denver. What did you hear about him while you were at Hidden Hills?"

"J-just that he was a traitor. He killed an army ranger, pushed Asher…Lieutenant Knight off a cliff and went AWOL—probably working with the insurgents he was secretly meeting."

"That's all garbage, all lies." Asher's muscles tightened until he felt like a coiled spring beside her. "Those shrinks at Hidden Hills manufactured my memories—whether you know that or not—to fit their story about Denver. It didn't happen that way. I don't know who shot the ranger, but it wasn't Denver, and he didn't push me. I slipped."

"How do you know that?" Tabitha's Adam's apple bobbed in her slender neck.

"Because Paige—" Asher slung an arm around her shoulders and pulled her close "—my fiancée, hypnotized me."

Apparently, the only word Tabitha heard was *fiancée*, because she repeated it. "Fiancée? Fiancée?"

Enjoying the warmth of Asher's body next to hers even if it was for show, Paige rested her head against his arm. "The doctors at Hidden Hills didn't even tell Asher he had a fiancée. Don't you find that odd? Shouldn't they be doing everything in their power to help him regain his memories, including filling in the pieces of his life for him?"

"Maybe they didn't know about you." Tabitha scooted to the edge of the chair.

"If they had access to his army files, they knew about me."

"Of course they did." Asher curled his fingers into her upper arm. "Wives, fiancées, children, it's all there. Paige should've been contacted immediately after the incident—she wasn't."

"Paige." Tabitha gave her the once-over, her gaze sweeping from the top of her head to the toes of her boots. "You helped Asher escape."

"Of course."

"I was going to help you, Asher." Tabitha pinned her hands between her knees, raising her broad shoulders to her ears. "That's why I wouldn't allow them to shoot you up with a tracker. I was going to get you out of Hidden Hills."

"You had a strange way of helping me, Tabitha, keeping me drugged up and confused. Taking away my clothes." He shook his head. "I don't know if I can trust you."

Tabitha flung her arms out to the sides. "I came alone. I tried to protect you."

The nurse opened her mouth again and snapped it shut.

Paige held her breath. Had she been about to repeat her proclamations of love and thought better of it?

Asher's nostrils flared. "How did you plan to protect me? And protect me from what? Why are they after me now, on whose orders and what are they going to do with me when they get me?"

"I was going to protect you by making sure they didn't take you back." Tabitha stood up but stayed close to the chair, her fingers brushing the padded arm. "I have a place, or my family does, not far from here. I was going to take you there. I didn't realize you had help...didn't realize you had a fiancée, but I can still take both of you there. You'll be safe. I already stocked it with food. You can stay hidden until..."

"Until what?" Asher turned his back on Tabitha. "I have to get to the bottom of this morass. I can't hide out forever. I have a life."

Tabitha plunged her hands into the pockets of her knee-length, black down coat. "It will at least give you some time out of the public eye to start making inquiries. Unless you start driving now, miles and miles away, you won't be able to get food. You can't show your face. You'll never know who to trust." She shuffled away from the chair. "Am I right, Paige? You know I'm right."

Paige hated to admit this woman with the slightly manic edge and a huge crush on Asher had a point, but she had a point. But the mania and the crush made it hard to trust her.

Without turning around, Asher dragged one hand

through his hair and said, "If you really want to help, Tabitha, go back to Hidden Hills and try to find out some information for me. I need to know what's behind the frame-up of Major Denver."

"I'm not sure I'd be safe if I returned to Hidden Hills." Tabitha inched closer to Asher's back, her body stiff.

A shaft of guilt lanced the back of Paige's neck, and she made a half turn toward the kitchen. "You must be hurting, and I never got you that water. I have some ibuprofen, too."

Now level with Asher, Paige ignored his eye roll and took another step toward the kitchen.

"I'd like that, Paige."

The breathless quality of Tabitha's voice made Paige take a quick glance over her shoulder.

In a blur, Tabitha lunged at Asher, her clenched fist raised.

Asher heard Tabitha's approach at the same time Paige screamed, "Look out."

Swinging around, his leg extended, Asher swept Tabitha's feet out from under her. She took a hard fall on her side, her head landing inches from the potbellied stove, her hand still fisted.

This time it was Paige's boot that came down on Tabitha's wrist…and she felt no sympathy. "What do you have in your hand?"

"Be careful, Paige." Asher crouched next to the nurse and pried open her fingers. He pinched the needle between his thumb and forefinger and held it up. "More sedation? This is how you're going to protect me? Who sent you?"

Tabitha's head whipped back and forth. "Nobody. I'm here on my own. You're not well. You have more drugs swimming in your body than you know. I can take care of you."

"Yeah, like some demented fan. What next? You're going to bash in his kneecaps?" Paige ground the toe of her boot against Tabitha's hand.

Asher's eyebrows shot up. "Paige, go check the mudroom for some rope."

"What are you going to do?" Tabitha's voice squeaked.

"You can't be trusted. That's the last time you try to inject some poison into my body."

"It's not poison, just a sedative, a mild sedative."

"In that case." Asher flicked his fingers against the glass tube of the syringe and plunged it into Tabitha's thigh, right through her jeans.

She gasped and her eyes widened.

The effect of the drug was instantaneous. Her mouth went slack, and her hand slid from her leg.

Paige covered her mouth. "Oh my God. If she'd stuck you with that thing, you would've been a goner and I would've been left alone with her."

"Eh." Asher nudged one of Tabitha's arms with the toe of his boot. "I think you could've taken her down."

"What now?" Paige hugged herself and rubbed her arms. "I don't want to be here when Tabitha comes to. I've heard enough from her."

"How do you think I felt being trapped in that place with her yammering in my ear night and day?"

"She thinks she's in love with you, Asher."

"She's just obsessed. This has nothing to do with love."

"We can't stay here now, and Tabitha was right about one thing." Paige scooped up a handful of wrappers. "We need to get out of this area so we can buy some food and other supplies."

"We also need a base where I can start investigating this conspiracy—against me and Major Denver." He jerked his head up. "And start getting my life back with you."

Paige swallowed. That always seemed like an afterthought for him that he had to throw in there for her benefit. "What are we going to do with Tabitha?"

"She said it wasn't poison. We'll keep her in front of the heater. Her car's out back and she can leave when she wakes up."

"Without you."

"Thank God, without me." Asher bent down on one knee next to Tabitha and dipped his hand into her jacket pocket.

"What are you looking for?"

"Anything—phone, keys, more drugs."

"Just watch out for any more syringes. You could poke your finger."

"I will." He dragged his hand from the pocket,

dangling a key chain from his finger. "Looks like car keys, house key, cabin key, so she wasn't lying about that."

"How do you know that's a key to her parents' cabin?"

"Could be the piece of tape across the top that says 'cabin.'" He plucked one of the keys from the key chain and held it up.

"Are you thinking what I'm thinking?"

He raised one eyebrow. "Probably not."

Tilting her head at him, she said, "Tabitha said there was food there. Maybe we should raid her cabin before she comes to."

Asher slid the key from the ring and tossed it to her. "You can be in charge of cabin raiding. Did she say where it was located?"

"Have you found her phone yet? Maybe she has it on her phone's GPS."

"She had me on a GPS, why not the cabin?" He unzipped the other pocket and reached inside. "Nothing in here except a couple of bucks."

"Let's keep it. She owes you, big-time." Paige thrust out her hand, palm up.

Asher slapped the bills into her hand and then squeezed it. "I guess I must feel comfortable with criminals."

"What she stole from you is worth a lot more than a few bucks." Paige winked. "Besides, if she's so crazy in love with you, she won't mind."

Asher wagged a finger at her. "Justification. My dad had all kinds of excuses for his behavior."

Paige froze midway to stuffing Tabitha's money and key into the front pocket of her jeans. "He did? Do you remember that? Do you remember his excuses?"

Asher glanced up from rummaging through Tabitha's pockets, and a new light gleamed from his eyes. "I remember something. My mind flashed on a conversation with my father. I even saw him in my head."

"That's great news, Asher. Without all those drugs running through your system, you have a good chance of recovering your memories. What did he look like—your father?"

"A lot like me." He brushed his hand over the top of his short, brown hair. "Except no hair, shaved head."

Her heart did a little flip in her chest. "That's him. I've seen pictures of your father—handsome devil, handsome, crooked devil."

"That memory just came naturally to me in the course of our conversation. When I launched myself at the guy at the resort, I also recalled that Cam Sutton played football, too. Do you think that's how it's going to happen for me?"

"I think it's a great start."

He patted an inside pocket of Tabitha's jacket. "Phone. This could yield some important information."

"Like if her visit here was an outing planned for her by Hidden Hills?"

"Exactly." He tapped the phone. "Password protected."

"Let me have it. I have some ideas. If you were her obsession—and you were—her password might be easy to guess."

"You have no idea how that creeps me out."

"Your devastating charm and hunky good looks worked to your advantage in this case." Paige cupped the phone in her hand and started trying some obvious passwords. "Well, at least her password isn't your first name, last name or any combinations of those."

"That's a relief." He jingled Tabitha's car keys in his hand. "Since we can't access her phone right away, I'm going out to her car to see if she has anything in there, maybe directions to the cabin."

"Okay, I'll keep trying the phone's password in here where it's warm."

Asher went through the mudroom to the back, and Paige perched on a stool in the kitchen, wanting to keep as far away from Tabitha as possible. The woman could reanimate like one of those villains from a horror movie and grab her ankle.

She murmured to herself as she tried one password after another. "Delta Force, D-Boy, Lieutenant Asher."

Her finger hovered over the letters, and the back door crashed open. She jumped from the stool and spun around. Her heart slammed against her chest.

Asher charged from the mudroom and grabbed her arm. "Let's go. They're here."

Paige didn't ask one question. Curling her fingers around Tabitha's phone, she allowed Asher to drag her from the cabin as she couldn't keep up with his long stride.

The cold air hit her face and made her nose run instantly.

Asher still had her car keys, and he gave her a little push toward the passenger side. "Get in. I'm taking that small access road through these woods. It's our only chance. As soon as they hear this engine start, they'll know we're out here instead of inside."

Paige shut the car door without slamming it. As Asher hopped in beside her and shoved the keys in the ignition, she held her breath and twisted her head over her shoulder to watch for anyone coming after them.

In an instant a flash of light lit up the night sky. The cabin exploded behind them. They didn't want to capture them... They wanted to kill them.

Chapter Eight

Asher cranked the engine and floored it, navigating between two tall pines that ushered in the access road behind the cabin.

The people after them would never hear it. The explosion and fire would mask any sounds from the car.

The flames shot up toward the clouds, and Paige dug her fingers into Asher's arm as the car bounced over the rough road. "Tabitha!"

"She's dead, Paige. Did you get a look at that inferno?"

She covered her face with both hands. "Oh my God. They thought we were in there. They don't care to get you back anymore. They just want to kill you."

"Us." He clenched his jaw. "They want to kill *us*."

"How did you know someone was there?"

"I heard an engine when I was going through Tabitha's car. I peeked around the corner of the cabin and saw a vehicle pulling into the driveway. I knew it had to be trouble, but I had no idea they were going to firebomb the cabin—with Tabitha in it."

"If you hadn't gone out to her car, it would've been

us in there." She cranked her head over her shoulder. "Do you think they're coming after us?"

"I don't think so. They figured we were inside, and now they think we're burning to a crisp." He tightened his hands on the steering wheel as they hit another bump. "That fire saved us. If they'd been about to surround the cabin, they would've heard the car. They would've known we survived the blast. Instead they think they caught us off guard."

"If they think we're both dead, it does buy us some time. They're not going to be hanging around waiting for the fire department to find out how many dead bodies are in the cabin. They probably won't even stay long enough to check out the cars in the back."

"A flying, burning log crashed through the windshield of Tabitha's car as we pulled away. It's probably burning as we speak. Maybe it even exploded."

Paige twisted in her seat to stare out the back window. "I see a lot of black smoke billowing up into the air. If they left right away, will we meet them on the main road?"

"We'll wait before we hit the road, see if any cars pass by. Watch for the emergency vehicles."

"Then what?"

"We're going to Tabitha's family's cabin."

"What?" She turned to stare at him.

"Before I heard the engine from the road, I found the address to the cabin in Tabitha's car's GPS. Then I wiped it clean, although the fire may have done a better job of that."

"Do you think it's safe to go there now? Even if we don't have to worry about Tabitha showing up—" Paige's voice hitched in her throat "—the people she worked with must know her family has that cabin. Once her family hears about her death, they'll probably head out this way, too. It all sounds risky."

"If the people after us think we died in that fire, they're not going to be looking for us in Tabitha's cabin or any other cabin. Since the cabin that just blew up was not Tabitha's, the arson investigators are not going to be able to identify the body immediately. They'll most likely have to use dental records, and that's even if someone reports Tabitha missing. Do you think Hidden Hills is going to report one of its nurses missing if its employees are the ones responsible for her death? Not likely. Tabitha's cabin is our safest bet right now. Nobody's going to be looking for us right away, and nobody's going to be looking for her. We need to stay out of sight for now."

Paige settled back in her seat and held her hands splayed in front of her. "Yep, still shaking."

"My God. That was close. If I hadn't gone out to Tabitha's car and heard the approaching engine, we would've still been inside that cabin when they firebombed it."

"How did they know Tabitha was there? Do you think she lied and was working with them all along?"

"Nope."

"You trust her?" Paige clasped her hands in her lap to stop their trembling.

"I trust nothing and no one but solid evidence.

After I located the GPS information, I searched the outside of Tabitha's car and found a tracking device stuck to the undercarriage."

"So, Tabitha was following you using a GPS on your hospital gown and the friendly docs at Hidden Hills were following Tabitha with a GPS on her car." Paige raised her folded hands to her lips, pressing them against her white knuckles.

Asher clicked his tongue. "I'm gonna give the love-struck Tabitha the benefit of the doubt here and assume she didn't know about the tracker. They used her."

"She led them right to us…and to her own death." Paige shivered, and her teeth chattered. "If Tabitha hadn't been conked out, she could've gotten out with us."

Asher clasped her knee with his warm hand. "That's not our fault. She came to the cabin to sedate me, and God knows what she would've done to you once she had me under."

The car slowed down as they approached the main road. Asher pulled over on the access road with a view of the action and idled, headlights out. "Let's see what's what before continuing."

Paige cracked her window a few inches. "I think I hear sirens."

The wails got louder and louder until the emergency vehicles passed before them on the main road.

Asher threw the car into gear. "The people who started the fire have already left. Tabitha's cabin is just a few miles ahead off another access road."

Paige didn't relish the thought of staying in the cabin Tabitha had planned for her and Asher's love nest, but if she could turn it into a love nest for the two of them instead, she could live with it.

She slid a glance toward Asher. He'd remembered details about his father and Cam. Details about her and their daughter couldn't be far behind. She'd been ready to tell him about Ivy right before Tabitha interrupted them.

Of course, once she told him they had a four-year-old together, she'd have to explain why it was they were engaged instead of married.

And right now she was enjoying his ignorance.

ASHER HUNCHED OVER the steering wheel when they arrived at Tabitha's cabin and peered through the windshield of the car. Although it looked deserted, he cut the lights and swung the car around the back.

He and Paige hadn't had two minutes together where they hadn't been under a threat or some kind of pressure. Maybe once he had a chance to catch his breath, the memories would start rolling in.

He wanted to give this woman what she wanted, what she deserved. He wanted to love her. Hell, he was already half in love with her now, even though she was a stranger.

He parked and held up his hand to her as she reached for the door handle. "Stay in the car until I give you the all-clear signal."

"Do you think it might be a trap?"

"It could be anything. Let me go first and check it out. This place looks bigger than the other one."

"I hope those owners had insurance. We're responsible for the destruction of their cabin."

"We didn't blow it up." He pinched her chin. "Wait here."

Asher crept up to the back door, on the lookout for cameras, dogs and laser trip wires. He made it to the door unaccosted and shoved the key into the dead bolt. When he heard the click, he relaxed his shoulders. At least they had the right place and the right key.

He opened the door and poked his head inside... listening. He stepped inside and the warmth of the cabin enveloped him. Moving through the cabin, he did a quick search and then went to the back door and waved to Paige.

He waited for her and swung the door wide. "This one looks a lot more comfortable than the previous cabin."

"That's because Tabitha had prepared it for you." Paige swept past him and made a beeline for the kitchen.

Cranking on a burner on the stove, she said, "The gas is turned on."

"And the fridge is stocked." He hung on the open refrigerator door, taking in the bottles of water, juice, wine, eggs, milk, vegetables—enough food to feed a family of six for a week.

Paige joined him, looking over his shoulder.

"Wine? She really had a cozy getaway planned for the two of you."

"Yeah, with me drugged out of my mind and strapped to a bed. That would've been worse than Hidden Hills."

"Do you want to eat something? I can cook a quick meal—scrambled eggs and toast, at least."

"It's late. You must be exhausted."

"Actually, I'm wired."

"Have a glass of wine—or two. I'll keep watch. I've had enough sleep to last me the next six months."

Two red spots formed on Paige's cheeks, and she pressed one hand against her chest. "I—I don't drink."

"Maybe there's some hot tea instead." He flung open a cupboard door and looked over his shoulder. "Do I?"

"Do you drink?"

"Isn't that strange? I don't even know what I like and don't like." He shrugged and swept a box of tea bags from the shelf.

"You do drink sometimes, but we don't drink together. It's not something we do."

"I need to keep my wits sharp, anyway. At least as sharp as they can be under the circumstances." He shook the box of tea. "Do you want a cup?"

"No, thanks. I'll scope out the sleeping arrangements, unless you think we should stay down here." She tipped her head back and surveyed the loft above them.

"You can check it out upstairs, but I'll definitely

be bunking down here. Do you want me to get your bags from the car?"

"Please. I'd like to get on my laptop and see if there's any news."

"It's a lucky break we didn't bring your stuff into the first cabin. It would've all been destroyed."

"Along with Tabitha."

"Are you all right, Paige? Are you sure you don't want some tea? You still look rattled." He strode to a couch in the room and dragged a blanket from the back of it. "Why don't you lie down? I'll bring you your laptop."

"You're the patient here. I'm taking care of you, remember?"

"I do remember." He shook out the blanket and placed it on the couch. "And you did a helluva job, but I'm getting better and better, so you can take a break."

"Maybe we can both take a break."

"I'm more than ready." Asher left Paige standing next to the couch and returned to the car. The stillness of the air and the gray skies signaled snow on the way. Soon the resort would be crawling with skiers and snowboarders, and they'd be just two more people holed up in a mountain cabin.

He gathered Paige's bag and laptop case from the back seat of the car and brought them back to the cabin.

He dropped the bags on the floor and jerked back as Paige faced him holding a shotgun. "Are you pointing that at me?"

"Of course not. I found it in the closet." She leaned it against the stone mantel. "It might come in handy though."

"You don't look relaxed at all." He grabbed the strap of her laptop case and hauled it over his shoulder. "Do you think they have Wi-Fi here?"

"My phone has a connection. I'm sure all the lodges and hotels have service, so it makes sense they'd have it out here."

He swung the case onto the coffee table. "Give it a try. I want to start doing a little research tomorrow."

"Research?" She leaned forward and pulled her computer from its case.

"On Major Denver. I want to see what the official story is. You must know all my Delta Force teammates, right? I want to try to contact them. They wanted nothing to do with me once I implicated Denver."

"That's what the mad scientists at Hidden Hills told you, anyway. You can't be sure they even contacted your teammates, other than to tell them you survived."

"If they had, and I had made contact with them, would they have told me about you?" He collapsed in the chair across from the sofa and studied her face, which seemed to take on a guarded look.

"Yes, of course. I've met all your team members, including Major Denver." She pointed at him and circled her finger in the air. "Do you still suspect me of being a fake fiancée?"

"I never suspected that. At least I don't think I

did. There was something about you from the very beginning when I stumbled on you in the woods."

He drew a cross over his heart as she began to protest. "Honest. I'm not just telling you what you want to hear, and then your actions backed up my initial instincts. You rescued me."

She waved her hands in the air, as if fanning her hot cheeks. "Believe me, that's a switch for us. I'm usually the one in need of saving."

He stretched his legs in front of him, propping them on the coffee table between him and Paige. "You sure you don't want to try some of that hocus-pocus on me tonight?"

"I think you've had enough for one night. We both have." Her fingers flew across her laptop's keyboard. "I don't see anything about the fire, but then I'm not quite sure where to look online for local news."

"You don't see anything about a soldier going AWOL from a rehabilitation center, do you?"

She snorted. "Some rehabilitation center, but no, nothing about that, either."

"Any stories about Major Denver?" Despite his interest in her answer, Asher yawned and stretched his arms over his head.

"That story is top secret, not for public consumption. I only know about it because the army told me when they were explaining your incident to me."

"I imagine my situation will stay under the radar, too."

"I'm keeping you from your bed." She scooted off the edge of the sofa. "Unless you want the loft."

"It's best if I stay down here, and now I have a weapon." He jerked his thumb at the rifle leaning against the fireplace. "You go upstairs and try to get some sleep once you're done on the computer."

"I do want to check some emails just in case my clients are having any difficulties."

"I'm sure you left them in good hands. You'd be that kind of therapist."

She peered at him over the top of her computer. "Don't go putting me on a pedestal. You'll be sorely disappointed."

"I will keep my expectations low and my teeth clean, thanks to you leaving that other bag in the car." He stood up and reached for the ceiling. "The only things we lost in that cabin were my hospital gown and some food and water."

"And Tabitha."

"I know." He came around the back of the sofa and placed his hands on her shoulders. Her soft hair tickled the backs of his hands. "I don't mean to sound callous, but I don't think Tabitha had anything good in store for either of us."

"I know. I just…" She flicked her fingers at him. "Go brush your teeth. I'll vacate your bed in a few minutes."

He snatched up the bag containing the toiletries Paige bought him and crumpled it in his fist. He didn't want Paige to vacate his bed, but sleeping together tonight would only emphasize the awkwardness of their situation.

Maybe it was too much to ask, but he wanted their

love and relationship to develop naturally as he began to recall things, not to have an insta-fiancée because it was part of some life he couldn't remember.

In one dark corner of his mind he couldn't banish the thought that just because he'd been in love with Paige once didn't mean he was going to remember that love, and they'd be back in the same place.

Was that what she feared, too? Something was spooking her about him recovering his memories. Why wouldn't she just jump right in and tell him everything about their life together?

After brushing his teeth, he wiped his mouth on the clean towel Tabitha had provided. As he hung it back up, a gasp from the other room caused him to miss the rack and drop the towel on the floor.

Asher bolted from the bathroom. "What's wrong?"

"I got an email from one of your Delta Force teammates."

"That's good, isn't it?" His eager stride ate up the space between them, and he crowded next to her on the sofa.

"Not—" she shoved the computer onto his lap "—necessarily."

As he scanned the words on the screen, he read them aloud. "'If you know where that traitorous SOB is hiding, you can tell him to rot in hell.'"

Chapter Nine

Asher's eyebrows shot up. "That's kinda harsh, isn't it?"

Paige clicked her tongue. "That's Cameron Sutton—opens his mouth before he thinks anything through."

"Cam." Asher rubbed the stubble on his chin. "That sounds thought-out to me—and decisive. It's what they must all be thinking, isn't it? Cam just put voice to it."

"He must know you left Hidden Hills."

"If he knew I was there at all." Asher drew his brows together. "I don't like him calling you out though."

"No offense taken." She reached past him and wiggled her fingers over the keyboard. "Should I give him the good news?"

"Wait." He cinched her wrist with his fingers. "I'm assuming your laptop isn't encrypted or secure in any way, besides your password. Someone, somewhere may be waiting for some communication from your email. They might be able to track you down, or at least know you're still alive. It's too soon."

She snatched her hands back and pressed one to the side of her head. "You're not kidding, are you? Someone might be monitoring my email."

"I'm erring on the side of safety. No reason to tip off anyone that we're still alive when the minions from Hidden Hills think we were in that cabin." He held up a finger. "Cam is feeling chatty."

Draping an arm over his shoulder, she leaned toward the laptop, her soft breast pressing against his arm. "He said he's found evidence that Denver was set up."

"Him and me both." Asher trailed his finger across Cam Sutton's words. "Says he has proof the emails that first implicated Denver were planted."

Paige drummed her fingers on the laptop as they waited for more from Cam, but the next email to make it through was an ad for online coupons.

"I think Cam's exhausted all his words for now." Paige sighed. "I wish I could call him. Would that be safe?"

"Nope."

She slid a gaze to her phone charging on the table. "You mean they could be tracking my phone, too?"

"They could get your number and ping it. They can look at your calls. Any call coming from your phone right now wouldn't look good for us."

"We're going to be holed up in here with no communication with anyone."

"It doesn't mean I can't do a little research on your laptop." He flicked a finger at the screen. "And if we can pick up a temp phone, we could make that call to Cam."

She snapped her fingers. "Every mom-and-pop grocer carries phones these days. I'm sure I could venture out tomorrow in some kind of disguise and find a phone."

"We'll figure it out." He handed the computer back to her and pushed up from the sofa, away from Paige's warmth. "It's late. This day started a long time ago."

"I know." She logged off her laptop and scrambled from the sofa. "I can see a bathroom upstairs. I'll head up to the loft, brush my teeth and hit the sack. I haven't even been up there yet."

Backing up, Asher tilted back his head. "There's at least one bed up there and what looks like a sleeper sofa next to the bathroom. I'll keep watch down here."

"You need your sleep, too. We could take turns keeping watch."

"Okay, I'll take the first shift."

She put a foot on the bottom step and wedged her hand on her hip. "You don't fool me for one minute, Asher. Your shift would never end and mine would never begin."

"Don't worry about it. You've done enough worrying about me. I'm fine, and I'll be better once I figure out what the hell is going on."

Paige tossed her head and jogged up the stairs. Her voice floated down. "Wow, you're not gonna believe what's up here."

Asher's hand clenched reflexively. "Something bad?"

"Depends on your perspective." Paige leaned over the loft's railing and dropped something over.

Pink rose petals floated to the floor, a few landing on his shoulder. He brushed them off. "Dead flowers?"

"Tabitha was getting ready for your visit. Rose petals on the bed, candles all over the room—" a drawer opened and slammed "—condoms in the nightstand drawer."

Asher whistled. "That woman was seriously delusional. I feel sorry for her now."

"I know. I almost feel like a voyeur pawing through all this stuff—evidence of her obsession. Apparently, she also has an obsession for cats, unless this cat theme is her parents' idea of great cabin decor."

"On the plus side, you can now sleep on rose petals." Asher grabbed the shotgun, saw it was loaded and stationed it on the floor next to the sofa. "I thought you wanted your laptop with you."

"I'm tired. I'm going to sleep—without the rose petals. I shook them off the bedspread."

The light went off in the loft, and Asher turned off the lamp next to the sofa. "Good night, Paige. Thanks for rescuing me."

"Good night, Asher. Glad to return the favor."

He pulled the blanket up to his chin and closed his eyes as he inhaled the sweet scent Paige had left behind.

He didn't need rose petals, but he was beginning to realize he needed Paige—if she'd only help him remember.

THE NEXT MORNING, Paige rolled from the bed and padded to the window. Her gaze followed the puffs of snow as they fell from the gray sky and kissed the branches of the pines.

Snow meant people flooding the area, not that she and Asher could stay in this cabin forever hanging on to some sort of suspended thread of time. Asher had to get his life…and his memories back.

The smell of coffee wafted up to the loft, and Paige turned away from the window. She crossed the room and hung over the railing. "The coffee smells good. I'll make some breakfast to go along with it."

Asher shuffled backward out of the kitchen, his head tilted back. "I took care of breakfast. Pancakes."

"Ooh, I'll be right down." Paige tugged at the hem of her nightshirt—hardly sexy, but should she change into clothes? She smoothed the material over her thighs and headed for the stairs. That man downstairs was her fiancé—whether or not he remembered.

She pulled a stool up to the counter as Asher put a plate in front of her stacked with pancakes.

He held up a bottle in each hand. "We even have a choice of maple syrup or blueberry syrup."

"What's a visit to Vermont without maple syrup?"

He shoved the bottle toward her. "You should check out the local news on your laptop. I'm curious as to what the authorities are calling that fire at the cabin and if they've discovered Tabitha's body yet."

"If they report just one body in the cabin, we're going to have to get moving. The people after us are going to realize we weren't in the cabin."

Asher stabbed his fork into four layers of pancakes. "But it felt good to slow down and now it feels good to eat some real food."

"Did you sleep okay on the sofa?" She jerked her thumb over her shoulder at Asher's bed for the night.

"I probably had my best night of sleep since the incident."

"You didn't keep watch? I noticed the rifle was your sleeping companion." She knew she wasn't.

"I'm a light sleeper, especially now. I figured I could catch some shut-eye, and if anyone tried to break in, I'd wake up."

"So, on the agenda today—pack up and get out of here, get a burner phone and call Cam—" she tilted her head to the side "—and maybe get you a few more clothes."

"If you say so. I'd rather pack up some of this food Tabitha put aside for our rendezvous." He licked some syrup from his lips. "And I'm ready for another hypnosis session when you are. This time, I want to know everything that happened in my life *before* that hillside in Afghanistan."

"Maybe tonight when we get settled somewhere." She made little crosses in the syrup on her plate with the tines of her fork. "Where *are* we headed? I suppose it's not a good idea to go back to Vegas. They'd look for us there."

"I'd like to stay close to the action, close to DC. I can't exactly waltz into army headquarters somewhere and tell them my memory of the incident with Major Denver was a lie and try to correct the story. I need to know who's behind the machinations at Hidden Hills, who wanted that version of the story to come out."

"You have to be careful, Asher. Whoever is behind that story is one hundred percent invested in it. We both know this whole thing was not engineered by a couple of shrinks at Hidden Hills. They had orders."

"I wonder how high up the chain of command this goes." He dropped his fork on his plate and swept it from the counter. "I think Cam Sutton can help."

"As soon as we tell him you're not a traitorous SOB."

"The kid has a hard head, but his heart's always in the right place."

Paige pressed two fingers to her lips. Asher's memories and feelings were seeping in naturally.

Asher dropped their plates in the sink with a crash. "How about that? I remembered that about Cam's personality."

"I noticed. It'll all come back to you in time without the interference from the Dr. Frankensteins at Hidden Hills and their cocktail of drugs."

Asher dried his hands on a paper towel and then leaned across the counter and traced the edge of her jaw with one fingertip. "I knew you, too, Paige. When I first saw you in the woods, I knew I could trust you."

"That'll all come back to you, too—all of it." She blinked her eyes and pasted a smile on her face. "If you don't mind, I'm going to take a shower first and get dressed. I have more to pack than you."

"Would you mind checking the news on your computer first? Then I'll clean up in here, put everything back the way we found it—except the food. I'm taking what we can."

"Tabitha bought it for you, anyway." Her stomach dropped and she flattened one hand against it. She still couldn't quite believe they'd left a dead body behind in that cabin.

Crossing his arms over his chest, Asher wedged his hip against the counter. "Tabitha was playing with fire, Paige. She was a nurse. As a mental health professional, would you have gone along with some crazy scheme to imprison a soldier who'd just been through a trauma? Trick him?"

"No way."

"Like I said, playing with fire."

Paige unplugged her laptop and brought it to the counter. "What do you think? Vermont news? News for this ski resort?"

"I'd enter the name of the resort."

Paige typed in the resort name. The screen populated with weather reports and ski conditions, and then she saw it. "Cabin fire. They have it."

His hands in the sink washing dishes, Asher glanced over. "What does it say?"

"They think it's arson." She traced a finger across the words of the brief article. "Nothing about a body."

"I can't believe the firefighters didn't find her. They're just not reporting anything yet, or maybe just not in that article. Is there anything else?"

Paige clicked for the next screen of search results. "I don't see anything else."

"Then the people who set the fire don't know, either." He draped the dish towel over the oven door handle. "And that gives us a little time."

Paige blew out a breath. "I'm going to take that shower now."

"Don't use all the hot water." He threw open a cupboard door. "I'm going to get some supplies for the road. The less we have to stop in at stores around here, the better."

Paige showered and got dressed in record time. She didn't like being here in Tabitha's cabin—and it wasn't just because she feared being tracked. The whole place gave her the creeps.

She stomped on one of the dried rose petals. They needed to get out of here.

By the time she got downstairs, dragging her suitcase behind her, Asher had packed up a few bags of food. He glanced up at her approach.

He pointed at her computer. "I took the liberty of looking up a few places nearby where we can get our hands on a phone, but it might be best to head to the capital. Finding a place to stay is going to be harder.

We don't have enough cash to book a hotel room, and we don't want to use your credit or debit cards."

"I might be able to get my hands on some cash."

"No banks."

"Where's your father when you need him?" She put a hand over her mouth as her eyes flew to his face. "I'm kidding. Y-you got to the point where we could joke about your father."

"I would hope so. I don't think a little amnesia has made me overly sensitive."

Paige watched Asher as he walked upstairs to take a shower. She hoped a little amnesia hadn't made him overly judgmental, either.

THE SNOW HAD stopped falling by the time they'd packed up everything they needed from Tabitha's cabin.

Asher crouched next to the back door and slid the key beneath the mat. "Tabitha's parents are going to wonder what she was doing in that other cabin when theirs was two miles away."

"They should be wondering why someone would want to kill their daughter."

"That investigation will go nowhere. The authorities will connect her to Hidden Hills, but the doctors there aren't going to reveal Tabitha's fascination with a missing, damaged soldier."

As Asher hoisted her suitcase into the trunk, she put a hand on his arm. "Is that how you see yourself? Damaged?"

"I'm not whole, am I? I won't be whole until I

remember everything, and I won't be whole until I figure out why Denver was set up." He handed her the keys. "You drive, and I'll navigate."

"Where to? Did you make a decision?"

"Head south, and we'll buy a phone as soon as it feels safe, more populated."

"Hopefully the whole bunch at Hidden Hills thinks we're dead and gone."

"For now. I'd still like to get out of this general area."

Paige accelerated in agreement. She wanted to put as many miles as possible between them and the burned-out cabin—and Tabitha's body.

About an hour later, Asher directed her to take one of the turnoffs for Montpelier. "Not a huge city, but we're not going to stand out, either."

Paige pulled into the parking lot of a big multipurpose store. "We can get a phone here, clothes and even more food."

"Are you going to use your cash for this or use that card again?"

"I'm going to retire the credit card now. Back in Mooseville, once I decided I was going to break you out of that hellhole, I made two visits to the ATM over two days and took as much money as I could out of my...our savings." She patted her purse. "I have enough for this shopping spree, anyway."

"And the rest? You mentioned before you could get your hands on some cash—without robbing a bank."

"My mother's...friend. He was Dad's army buddy,

and he and Mom have been spending a lot of time together. I think they're a couple. They just haven't admitted it to me yet. Anyway, Terrence is the one who found out where the army was keeping you. I think he could get us some cash."

"He's not going to be loyal to the army?"

"Are you loyal to the army after what they did to you and Major Denver? Terrence is loyal to me and my mom. He's going to do whatever it takes to protect me…and you."

They wandered around the store, picking up a temporary phone and a few more items of clothing for Asher.

As she stood beside Asher in the checkout line, with some cheap jeans and a few flannel shirts draped over his arm, Paige covered her smile with one hand.

He lifted his eyebrows. "What's wrong?"

"In the real world, you wouldn't be caught dead in those duds. You're a very sharp dresser—one of the good things you learned from your father."

He held the clothes away from his body and inspected them. "Even more reason for me to stay alive—so I can wear my own clothes again."

When they got to the car, Asher ripped into the phone. "We need to find a coffeehouse to charge this thing up and start making a few calls."

"We seem to be in a commercial area, should be able to find something around here."

A half mile out of the parking lot, Asher pointed at the windshield. "Up there on your right."

She parked in front of the coffeehouse, and they found a seat inside. While they sipped their coffee, they let the phone charge up.

Digging her own dead phone from her purse, she said, "I'm going to have to turn this on to get Cam's phone number."

"That should be okay. If our enemies do decide to ping your phone later, we'll be long gone from this location."

Paige swallowed. "Enemies?"

"What would you call them? These people are trying to kill us."

"Yeah, enemies will work." She powered up her phone and went to her contacts. "Might as well jot down all these numbers and program them into the new phone. I don't have anyone's number memorized anymore."

"Neither do I."

As she shot him a glance, he cracked a smile. The first she'd seen from him since Hidden Hills. She smacked his biceps, still hard and ready, with the flat of her hand

"If the army doesn't want you back, maybe you can have a career as a stand-up comedian."

"The army had better want me back." He tapped the table in front of the burner phone. "It's charged."

Leaving the phone plugged in, Paige took a deep breath and entered Cam's phone number. "He's probably not going to pick up from an unknown number."

"Probably not." Asher picked up the phone. "Let me leave the message."

He paused for several seconds and shook his head. "Cam, this is Asher. I'm with Paige and heard your message about me. I'm retracting my version of the events that led to Major Denver going AWOL. I was set up just as surely as he was and we need to talk."

Asher paused and rubbed his eyes. "Give us a call back at this number. It's a phone...a burner phone."

He broke off, and Paige studied his face. A light sheen of sweat glistened on Asher's forehead.

His jaw worked and he started talking again. "Trying to keep Paige's phone off. Long...long sto—"

"Asher!"

His eyes rolled back in his head. The phone slipped from his grip and fell to the floor...just before he hit the table.

Chapter Ten

Paige looked around the coffeehouse, her gaze darting from the occupied tables to the people standing in line. Thank God for people's addiction to their phones. Nobody had noticed Asher collapsing at the table.

Leaning forward, Paige swept the phone from the floor and then pretended she was talking to Asher—just in case someone looked up from texting long enough to notice.

Cam's voice mail was probably still recording, so she whispered into the phone. "Cam, it's Paige. Asher just collapsed. I'm going to need some help. We're in Vermont… Montpelier, but probably not for long."

She ended the call and folded her arms on the table, resting her chin on her hands. With her lips close to Asher's ear, she whispered, "What's wrong, Asher? Can you hear me?"

He answered with a soft moan. At least he wasn't dead.

What *had* happened? Had someone poisoned the coffee? She popped the lid off her own cup and eyed the liquid as she swirled it around. Nobody could've poisoned their coffee but the barista, and she doubted the doctors at Hidden Hills had compromised a couple of baristas in Montpelier.

Maybe he was just ill, still suffering from his head injury. God knew what kind of treatment he received for his physical injuries. Those doctors had been more concerned with his psychological responses—and how to tweak them.

She brushed his hair back from his clammy forehead. She couldn't risk calling 911 for him, but she couldn't risk not calling. She'd rather see him back at Hidden Hills than dead, although another stint at Hidden Hills might end in his death.

"Think." She pressed her fingers to her temples. She'd helped more than a few drunks out of bars. Could this be any different?

She grabbed Asher's wrists. "We're getting out of here. I'm going to help you, but you're walking out of here. Got it?"

Asher's eyelids fluttered and he moved his lips.

"I'm gonna take that as a yes." She shoved the phone in her purse and strapped it across her body. She crouched beside Asher's chair and dragged his arm over her shoulders.

"On the count of three, I'm going to straighten up and you're coming with me." She braced her feet on the floor. "One, two, three."

She pushed up and Asher made a move to join her, which made hoisting up easier than she thought. So, he could hear her and respond in some way.

"FAST FIVE" READER SURVEY

Your participation entitles you to:
※ **4 Thank-You Gifts Worth Over $20!**

Complete the survey in minutes.

Get **2 FREE** Books

Your Thank-You Gifts include **2 FREE BOOKS** and **2 MYSTERY GIFTS**. There's no obligation to purchase anything!

See inside for details.

Dear Reader,

Since you are a lover of our books, your opinions are important to us... and so is your time.

That's why we made sure your **"FAST FIVE" READER SURVEY** can be completed in just a few minutes. Your answers to the five questions will help us remain at the forefront of women's fiction.

And, as a thank-you for participating, we'd like to send you **4 FREE THANK-YOU GIFTS!**

Enjoy your gifts with our appreciation,

Pam Powers

To get your
4 FREE THANK-YOU GIFTS:

✴ Quickly complete the "Fast Five" Reader Survey
and return the insert.

"FAST FIVE" READER SURVEY

1 Do you sometimes read a book a second or third time? ○ Yes ○ No

2 Do you often choose reading over other forms of entertainment such as television? ○ Yes ○ No

3 When you were a child, did someone regularly read aloud to you? ○ Yes ○ No

4 Do you sometimes take a book with you when you travel outside the home? ○ Yes ○ No

5 In addition to books, do you regularly read newspapers and magazines? ○ Yes ○ No

YES! I have completed the above Reader Survey. Please send me my 4 FREE GIFTS (gifts worth over $20 retail). I understand that I am under no obligation to buy anything, as explained on the back of this card.

❏ I prefer the regular-print edition
182/382 HDL GM34

❏ I prefer the larger-print edition
199/399 HDL GM34

FIRST NAME

LAST NAME

ADDRESS

APT.#

CITY

STATE/ PROV.

ZIP/POSTAL CODE

Offer limited to one per household and not applicable to series that subscriber is currently receiving.
Your Privacy—The Reader Service is committed to protecting your privacy. Our Privacy Policy is available online at www.ReaderService.com or upon request from the Reader Service. We make a portion of our mailing list available to reputable third parties that offer products we believe may interest you. If you prefer that we not exchange your name with third parties, or if you wish to clarify or modify your communication preferences, please visit us at www.ReaderService.com/consumerschoice or write to us at Reader Service Preference Service, P.O. Box 9062, Buffalo, NY 14240-9062. Include your complete name and address.   HI-817-FF18

Once on her feet, Paige began to shuffle toward the door. A couple walking in gave them a wide berth but held the door open.

Paige nodded her thanks and half dragged, half carried Asher across the threshold.

A young man jumped from his chair in the coffeehouse and followed them outside. "Do you need help? Is he sick?"

"Yes, he's sick. I just need to get him to the car."

"Should I call 911?"

"No. He has the flu. I just need to get him home."

"I'll help you."

The man got on the other side of Asher and together they dragged him to the car and loaded him into the passenger seat.

The customer's friend had run out after them— too late to be of any help.

Paige rushed around to the driver's side. "Thanks so much."

Before she closed her door, she heard the man's friend say, "What's wrong with him?"

The man who'd helped her snorted, "Junkie."

As she slammed the car door, anger burned in Paige's chest—for just a second. Could it be a drug in Asher's system? Something put there by the Hidden Hills's doctors earlier to release at a later time? Was that possible? Something Tabitha had given him to make sure he'd stay compliant?

She snapped Asher's seat belt across his body and checked his breathing—still steady.

She drove out of the parking lot, just in case someone at the coffee place got the bright idea to call the cops or an ambulance.

She pulled up next to a park, its swings and slides deserted in the chilly air.

Could Asher be on something he hadn't told her about? She wouldn't blame him if he were after what he went through, but he had a strong aversion to drugs of any kind.

She pulled her old phone from her purse, turned it on and scanned through her contacts until she found Elena Morelli's number. As Paige didn't have the authority to prescribe medication, she often referred clients who needed drugs to Elena, a psychiatrist who worked in the same building.

Paige almost sobbed with relief when Elena picked up after the second ring.

"Hi, Paige. I thought you were out of town."

"I am. I need your help."

"I'm great. How are you?"

"I'm sorry, Elena. This is urgent."

"Shoot."

"I'm with a…friend, and he passed out. I think it might be some kind of narcotic, but I'm not sure. I need to know the best way to bring him out of this if it is a drug. Is there any such thing as a timed-release drug? Something injected that takes effect later?"

"Whoa." Elena whistled. "You just gave me a lot to chew on. Why not bring this friend to the emergency room? You're not in trouble, are you, Paige? Are you in a…situation?"

This could certainly be called a situation, but it wasn't the kind Elena meant.

"I'm fine, Elena. But my friend… It's a long story. I can't bring him to the hospital right now. I just want to make sure he's okay and see if there's anything I can do to speed up his recovery."

"I can't be much help if I don't know what drug he took. How's his breathing?"

"Steady, slow."

"Is his skin dry to the touch? You know what I mean? Parched?"

Paige shoved up Asher's sleeve and rubbed his forearm. "Doesn't seem to be."

"Peel up his eyelids. How do his eyes look? Bloodshot? Pupils dilated?"

Paige shoved back her seat so she could turn and face Asher in the passenger seat. Placing her thumb against his eyelid, she pushed it up. "His pupils are dilated."

"You don't have any idea what he took? Does he have anything on him?"

"It's not like that, Elena. He was drugged, but there's no way someone could've slipped him something before he passed out. That's why I asked about a timed-release drug."

"This is too weird, Paige. What kind of trouble are you in? Do you need to call someone in the program?"

"No. I'm fine, Elena. I just want to help my friend."

Elena took a measured breath over the phone.

"The best thing you can do for your *friend* right now is get him comfortable, lying down, preferably. Let him sleep it off, keep him on his side. When he starts to come to, and he will, give him lots of water and then get him to a Narcotics Anonymous program."

Paige closed her eyes and breathed deeply through her nose. Elena wasn't going to believe her anyway, so she might as well plunge right in. "So, is it possible to administer a delayed-reaction narcotic?"

"Yep, it's possible." Elena's clipped tones cut through the phone.

"Then that's what happened. How long could this last?" She couldn't have Asher passing out on her every twenty-four hours.

"I don't know. It depends on the drug. You're being totally serious, aren't you?"

"I am."

"You're going to have to take your friend to a doctor."

"I'll try." Paige brushed Asher's hair from his forehead and pressed her palm against it. "Thanks, Elena. If anyone asks if you've heard from me, tell them you haven't."

"Of course. Paige, are you okay?"

"I will be."

Paige ended the call. Where should they go? She didn't want to go back to Tabitha's cabin.

She pounded the steering wheel in frustration. The man who'd always helped her, the man with all the answers was now slumped in the seat next to her.

She shook her head. She'd had an idea before

how she could get cash. Using her own phone, she called Terrence, her father's best friend and now her mother's...best friend.

Asher stirred and mumbled.

"Asher?" Paige squeezed his shoulder. "Asher? Come out of it."

Terrence answered the phone, his voice sounding strong and sure—just what she needed. "Paige? Are you okay?"

"I'm fine, Terrence, but I do need to ask you another favor."

"I'm just about ready to head out for a three-day desert hike, Paige, but I'll do what I can."

What could he possibly do from the desert? "I need money—cash."

"Where are you? Still in Vermont?"

"Yes, but I can leave at any time." She took a side glance at Asher. Could she?

"Let me get on the phone with a couple of contacts out there before I leave." Terrence cleared his throat. "Did you see Asher?"

"He's with me, Terrence. I took him out of there."

"I'm assuming he didn't have their approval to leave if you need cash. How is he?"

"He's fine." She didn't want to worry her mother or Terrence. She'd put Mom through too much already. "We just really need that cash to get around without using my credit or debit cards."

"You *are* using your phone, Paige."

"Just to make a few calls. We have a temp phone."

"Then use it. Call me back on that phone later tonight and turn off the one in your hand. Do you have enough cash for tonight?"

"Yes."

"Good. Call me later—on that other phone."

She ended the call and powered off her phone. She dropped it in the cup holder and then started the engine. She had the cash right now to get them a hotel room. Asher had wanted to stay near DC, so she'd start driving south now.

Paige cast an anxious glance at Asher, still slumped in the passenger seat. He looked like he was asleep, but if he didn't come to soon, she'd have to take him to an emergency room—even if that meant he'd be recaptured.

Her muscles became more and more relaxed and her grip on the steering wheel looser and looser the farther she drove away from Hidden Hills.

Finally, as she sped out of Vermont, the temp phone rang. Keeping her eyes on the road, she felt for the phone and propped it on the steering wheel in front of her. Her heart jumped when she saw Cam's number.

"Cam, it's Paige. Don't hang up on me."

"Why would I hang up on you? I just called you back, or I thought I was calling Asher. Has he come to his senses?"

"Did you hear my part of the message?"

"I just heard Asher's message. What's going on?"

Paige slid a sideways glance at Asher. "Asher's in trouble. They've been messing with his mind, Cam."

"Can I talk to him?"

"H-he's out."

"Out? Out where?"

Paige scooped in a big breath. "He's knocked out, drugged, whatever. I don't know."

Cam let loose with a string of expletives. "What are you talking about? Is he still at that rehab center in Vermont?"

"I broke him out of there. They were the ones jerking him around, Cam. They're the reason he came out with that statement about Major Denver. The doctors at Hidden Hills planted those memories in his head."

"Paige, slow down. What's wrong with him now? He just left me a voice mail a few hours ago."

"If I had to guess, I'd say the docs at the rehab center injected him with some timed-release drug to try to control him. They didn't even tell him about me. They haven't been trying to help him at all. They only wanted him to tell their story about Major Denver."

"Unbelievable, but I know there's some setup involving Denver. I just learned that the original emails implicating him were bogus. Are you going to take Asher to the emergency room? Where are you, anyway?"

"We're on the road." She eased off the gas pedal. She didn't need to get pulled over for speeding now. "I don't want to take him to a hospital, Cam. I don't think he'd want that. It could lead to his recapture."

"Are you sure he's okay?"

Paige reached over and pressed her hand against Asher's chest, slowly rising and falling. "He's still breathing. He doesn't seem like he's in distress—no foaming at the mouth or jerking limbs."

"Well, that's a plus. Are you still in Vermont?"

"Just left it. Can you help me, Cam? Help us?"

"I'm leaving the country, Paige. You're gonna have to do this on your own. Can you do this on your own?"

She flushed and snapped, "Of course."

He clicked his tongue. "It sounds like you've been doing a great job so far… At least you got him out of Hidden Hills. Do you have money? A place to stay? You can't leave an electronic trail. You can't let the army track you down."

"I'm working on it. We're heading south. Before Asher…passed out, he told me he wanted to go to DC. He wants to figure out who's behind this."

"So do I. About how far are you from DC now?"

"Maybe another nine hours."

"I have an idea for you. My girl has a family home on Chesapeake Bay, about an hour outside the capital."

Paige blinked. "You have a girl?"

"Yeah, long story. It's her mother's home, but there's nobody there now. You and Asher can stay there and we can arrange to have money and resources there for you, including a doctor."

"Really? I would feel so much better if Asher could see a doctor."

"Martha has a lot of contacts in the area. We can do this as long as you can get Asher to Chesapeake in one piece. Can you do that, Paige? Can you do that without falling apart?"

If Asher's friends couldn't trust her, how could Asher with all his memories fresh in his mind?

She clenched her jaw and ground out the words. "I'm fine, Cam. I'm not falling apart. Just give me the address and I'll get Asher there if I have to die trying."

"Okay, okay."

Cam rattled off the address and instructions for getting a key. "Text me when you get there. And, Paige?"

"Yeah?"

"When Asher wakes up, tell him we have his back."

PAIGE DROVE ON into the late afternoon and the beginning of the evening. She listened to music, talked to herself, talked to Asher.

He stirred a few times, and she drove through a fast-food place to have food and water on hand when he woke up—because he *would* wake up.

Halfway through Delaware and the first verse of a song, she got her wish. Asher had been shifting his body for the past several miles, and now his eyelashes fluttered and he stretched his legs.

He mumbled and swiped the back of his hand across his mouth.

"Asher? Asher, are you awake?"

She couldn't wait to tell him the good news

about Cam and that they were on their way to a safe place—and she'd arranged it on her own.

He scooted up in his seat and rubbed his eyes, cranking his head back and forth as if to work the kinks out of his neck.

He muttered, "God," and then his hand closed around a water bottle in the cup holder.

Paige released a sigh. "*Thank* God. I was so worried about you, but I didn't call 911 and we're on our way to a safe house. You're even going to see a doctor there. There's food in the back, just burgers and fries, and we're halfway to DC."

Paige drew back her shoulders and waited for Asher to say more, maybe how he felt or what he thought happened to him.

Instead he downed the water and gazed out the window.

"Asher?" He seemed awake, but was this some kind of suspended state of consciousness? She waited for several minutes that stretched into an eternity.

"Asher? Did you hear me? We're on our way to a safe house." She touched his cool hand.

He snatched his hand away from her, screwed on the lid to the empty bottle, placed it back in the cup holder and finally turned toward her, his green eyes dark and unfathomable.

"When the hell were you going to tell me about our daughter?"

Chapter Eleven

Paige jerked the steering wheel, and the car swerved across an empty lane. She righted the car and hunched her shoulders.

"Y-you remembered? Everything?"

"Everything that matters." Asher's eyes narrowed, his jaw settling into a hard line.

"I thought piling that on when you still have unnamed forces after you…and your mind would be too much for you to handle."

"Really? Didn't you come out to Hidden Hills to see me so that you could help me get my memory back? Make me whole?"

"I did, but that was before I knew the full extent of what they were doing to you. I still don't know the entire story—and neither do you. I had to haul you out of that coffee place earlier because you just passed out. Do you remember that?"

"I remember leaving a message for Cam, and then…nothing."

"Exactly. Do you understand why I didn't think it was a great idea to tell you about Ivy?"

"Let's get real, Paige." He gripped his knees. "You didn't think it was a great idea to tell me about Ivy because you didn't want to reveal the circumstances of her birth and everything that followed."

Her nose stung, and she tried to swallow the lump in her throat. "Okay, maybe I thought that was too much for you to bear. You didn't remember me, didn't remember what I went through. I didn't want you to worry about putting your faith in a woman, a stranger really, who'd had…issues."

"Who was an alcoholic who relapsed after the birth of our child. An alcoholic who put that child in danger. An alcoholic I couldn't trust with my daughter."

The road swam before her, and she blinked her eyes, dislodging a tear from her lashes. "I could've told you the whole story about my recovery and my path to sobriety, but it would've just been words to you, hollow words if you couldn't remember the ups and downs and the feelings."

Closing his eyes, Asher ran a thumb between his eyebrows. "I remember. God, I remember."

She skimmed her clammy palms over the steering wheel. "So, you conked out, and when you woke up, your memory had returned? That's not the effect they'd counted on, I'm sure."

He sliced a hand in the air to cut her off. "How is Ivy? Who's taking care of her? Your mom?"

"Mom has her and Ivy's doing great. She misses her daddy. I kept telling her you were coming home soon—and then you went on that assignment with Major Denver."

"Do you have pictures on your phone? I want to see her. I want to talk to her."

"Of course." She tipped her chin toward her phone on the console. "My phone's there."

He grabbed it and then folded his hands around it. "We still shouldn't turn this on."

Paige licked her lips. She didn't want to tell him she'd used her phone to call Elena and Terrence. She'd fallen into old habits so easily…keeping things from him.

"I'm truly sorry, Asher. I… Maybe I wanted you to keep me on that pedestal for a few more days. It was wrong. I should've told you everything."

The words came to her lips easily and willingly. She'd spent years apologizing to Asher.

He rubbed his eyes. "I can't believe I didn't remember Ivy. She's everything to me."

"I know that." Paige dropped her lashes. "I promise I'll give you a complete update on Ivy, but what do you think happened in the coffeehouse? Had you experienced that before at Hidden Hills?"

"The only time anything like that occurred at Hidden Hills was the time I ran into you in the forest, when Granger and Lewis shot me with the dart. Complete blackout."

"Well, that didn't happen back in Montpelier. I keep thinking it must've been a timed-release drug. I called my friend Elena Morelli, a psychiatrist, and she told me there are such things."

"I can believe anything of those docs at Hidden Hills. If they can implant false memories in my brain, they can inject something into my system that will affect me later."

"But why would they do something like that?"

"Who knows?" He rubbed the back of his head where his dark hair was growing in over the wound. "If I had escaped and been on my own and collapsed like that in public, someone would've called 911 and they'd have me in their clutches again."

"I did the right thing not bringing you to an emergency room? I wasn't sure."

"You did the right thing." He cleared his throat. "Thanks."

She nodded her head, the pleasure in any compliment from him dulled by the knowledge that he resented her for keeping Ivy from him. Had she been wrong to want to bask in his pleasure at having a kickass fiancée who'd sprung him from captivity?

Even after she'd recovered from her addiction, she always looked for the acknowledgment of her weakness in Asher's eyes. She'd been sensitive to every nuance in his voice, every glance at her when she had Ivy in her arms.

Yeah, she'd been wrong. That hadn't been her call to make. She squared her shoulders. "I'm sorry. I should've told you everything about us and our daughter. I should've put you under hypnosis and brought you back—all the way back to the day we met at that party—when I was drunk and fell into the pool, fully clothed and clutching a margarita for dear life."

His lips twisted. "I still felt an overpowering urge to rescue you, drunk or not."

"And you did. You rescued me in every way imaginable." She covered one of his hands with hers. "I'm so glad you got your memory back."

"I am, too, but when am I going to pass out again and where? Maybe next time the drug will erase any memories I gained back and put me at square one." He pounded his knee with his fist. "I can't afford to be back at square one, Paige."

"I know that, but I meant what I said about the doctor."

"Doctor?"

Of course he couldn't remember what she'd said about their destination and the money and the doctor and Cam. He'd been remembering their whole tumultuous relationship together and what a bad mom she'd been.

"I talked to Cam—on the temp phone." She slipped her hand from Asher's and flicked on the windshield wipers. "We're heading to his girlfriend's place on Chesapeake Bay. They'll have money for us there and send a doctor over."

"Wait, wait." He held up his hands. "Maybe I don't have all my memories back. Cam Sutton has a girlfriend? A girlfriend with a place on Chesapeake Bay?"

"He told me it was a long story, so we didn't get into it. He also told me he's on his way out of the country, so maybe another deployment."

"I wonder where he's being assigned with Denver and me out."

"He didn't say, but the house will be empty. He gave me instructions. I also have Terrence working on getting us some cash."

"Terrence needs to be careful. He's retired. He doesn't need to be getting into any trouble with the army."

"He knows what he's doing. He has contacts in Atlantic City who might be able to help us out, too."

"You did good." Asher ran his fingers along her arm. "You saved me again."

"I think I owe you a lot of saves to pay you back for all the times you saved me."

He tapped the heel of his hand against his head. "It's a strange feeling knowing someone is controlling you remotely."

"Could your blackout have been a result of your injuries? You remembered everything when you woke up. Could it have been your body's way of healing you?"

"That sounds a lot better than some timed-release drug ready to bring me to my knees every twenty-four hours." He cocked an eyebrow at her. "How the hell did you get me out of that coffee place?"

"You were still on your feet. I half dragged, half carried you out." She winked. "Don't forget. I've had a lot of practice hauling drunks out of bars."

"You always were the best sponsor in AA."

"Full disclosure." She held up two fingers. "Another customer helped me through the parking lot and into the car."

"Another customer? Someone you could trust?"

"He wasn't going to turn around and call the police or EMTs, if that's what you mean. He thought you were a junkie." She bit her bottom lip.

"He's not so far from the truth." Asher thumped his fist against his chest. "I don't know what's coursing through my veins."

"Maybe Martha's doctor friend can figure it out."

"Martha?"

"Cam's girlfriend."

"Cam's girlfriend." He shook his head. "God help her."

Now that his memories had returned, Asher couldn't turn them off. Everything he and Paige had been through with her addiction to alcohol rushed back in every painful detail. He'd made it clear to her that she had to choose between him or the booze—she'd chosen the booze but then found out she was pregnant.

That had scared her. She'd stayed sober during her pregnancy but had fallen off the wagon after Ivy was born. He'd reached the end of the line with her, threatening to take the baby away from her unless she got help.

She loved Ivy as much as he did, and she got to work, with a vengeance—AA, therapy, cutting off drinking buddies. The process spurred her on to become a marriage, family and child counselor, and she attacked that course as vigorously as she had dealt with her addiction.

He understood why she'd want to keep all that from him a little while longer, but when he remembered he had a daughter and realized why she hadn't told him about Ivy, he'd gotten that sinking feeling in his gut—the same one he'd felt when Paige had tried to get sober the first time...and failed. She'd lied to him, hid things from him, made excuses. It had almost torn them apart—almost.

From the driver's seat, he glanced at her, head tipped to one side, mouth slightly ajar. They'd bonded over their dysfunctional family lives.

His father, a convicted bank robber serving time in federal prison, and hers, a disgraced cop who'd taken his own life, but her trauma had gone a step further.

As a teenager, Paige had found her father in the family's garage, his brains blown out. How did a kid recover from that? Paige had numbed it with alcohol.

Asher had dealt with his own...disappointment by becoming overly regimented in all aspects of his life. Fate had led him to Paige, just when she needed him and he needed her. Nothing could disrupt your life quite like an alcoholic.

Taking care of Paige had satisfied that driving need in his life to impose order on all things. It also taught him compassion and forgiveness—emotions that had been absent in his psychological makeup until that point. He needed to find those again.

Paige jerked awake, her eyes wide-open immediately. "Where are we?"

"We're already through Jersey. We have less than an hour to get there. Cam's girlfriend must be rolling in dough with an address like that."

"Cam said it's her mother's house."

"Where's the mom?"

"He didn't say, just that the house would be all ours."

"It'll be a good base for our operation, and now that the boys are back on my side, maybe I can get some help from them. I need to talk to Cam again and find out more about those emails he mentioned. I don't think my imprisonment had anything to do with me, and everything to do with Denver. I was just a tool for them."

Paige yawned. "Now that you have your memories back, do you remember anything more about the mission?"

"I remember the name of Denver's contact—Shabib. He had information for the major that he had to communicate in person. It was something Denver was expecting, something he'd been investigating—something big."

"Apparently, it was so big, he had to be neutralized."

"But they didn't get him, did they?" Asher watched the rain lash the windshield and the wipers flick the drops off as fast as they fell. "Denver's out there somewhere, and he's going to be counting on us—his team members—to help him."

"Where are you going to start?"

"At the beginning. I'm going to track down Shabib, one way or another."

"Turnoff in less than two miles." Paige hunched forward and peered through the rain. "This is an out-of-the-way place."

"The more remote, the better."

"The farther from Hidden Hills, the better."

"They're still probably trying to figure out what happened in that cabin."

Paige hugged herself and rubbed her arms. "I hate thinking about it."

"It all worked in our favor—fate."

"That was Tabitha's fate? To die in a fire in that cabin?"

"She etched it out herself." He aimed the car down a long driveway. "And this house on the bay is ours right now."

Asher slid out of the car and used the code on the garage door to open it. He drove the car into the garage and closed the door so it still looked like a deserted house.

Paige followed Cam's directions on the location of the key, and ten minutes later, they entered a lavishly decorated house, clean and well stocked with food.

Asher whistled as he hung on the fridge door and surveyed the contents. "We could probably hole up here for six months."

"Let's hope we don't have to." She kicked a duffel bag she dragged from beneath a chair. "Cash. I already called Terrence to let him know we had another source."

Asher shook his head. "I can't believe Cam orchestrated all this. He's not exactly a planner."

"I know, but his new girlfriend must be. He was on his way out of the country. Martha must've made these arrangements."

"We'll have to thank Martha if we ever meet her."

Paige looked up from pawing through the money in the bag. "Is that because you don't think they'll last…or you don't think we'll last?"

"Oh, I plan to be alive to meet any and all of Cam's girlfriends, and you're coming along for this ride. Speaking of staying alive—" he pointed at the duffel "—is the gun in there?"

She buried both hands in the bag and withdrew a .38, holding it by its barrel. "Just like Cam promised."

"I'm starting to revise my opinion of that hothead." Asher crossed the great room and took the gun from Paige. "Bullets?"

"I felt a box at the bottom of the bag."

"Money, weapon, food and your computer. I'm ready to get to work."

"I'm ready to go to sleep." Paige ran her hands through her hair. "And maybe take a shower."

"I'm ready to see pictures of Ivy." He raised his eyebrows. "You didn't think I forgot, did you?"

"Of course not." She retrieved her laptop and brought it to the kitchen counter. "I have a bunch from Thanksgiving. I sent some of those to you.

Those bastards at Hidden Hills must've seen them on your phone and still didn't bother to tell you about your daughter." Two red spots flared on Paige's cheeks. "I didn't, either."

"Two different motivations."

"Both selfish."

"No argument from me." Asher felt the anger tighten in his chest again and filled his lungs with air. At least he understood Paige's motivation, and it wasn't like she planned to keep Ivy's existence a secret from him forever. She'd just wanted a little breathing room away from his judgment and censure.

He joined her at the counter as she powered on the computer. "I never had my phone, anyway."

"They never gave you your phone?" Her fingers clicked across the keyboard. "Of course they didn't."

"My phone was never recovered—at least that's what they told me."

"Do you believe them?" She double-clicked a folder on her desktop and his daughter came back to him in living color.

He put his face close to the monitor and traced a finger around Ivy's face. "How could I have ever forgotten this cute little button?"

"You didn't have a choice." She clicked open another folder. "Here are the ones from Thanksgiving, which are on a phone somewhere in Afghanistan."

"Yeah, I wonder where it really is."

They spent the next fifteen minutes looking at pictures while Paige updated him on Ivy's latest antics. But he remembered these photos now, remembered that Ivy had started singing into a hairbrush, had her first ballet recital, was begging for a puppy.

Paige was a good mom and even across the miles had kept him informed about Ivy's activities.

Guilt tweaked the edges of his mind. She kept him apprised of every detail because she still felt as if she had to prove herself to him. Prove that she was a good mother.

No wonder she'd wanted a brief respite from his accusing eyes.

He turned to her suddenly and cupped her face with one hand. "You're doing a great job with Ivy. She looks happy and healthy. And all this... You did this. You got us here to safety."

Paige's lips curved into a smile. "Technically, Cam and his girlfriend got us here."

"Cam's not here. You are." He brushed his thumb across her lips. "You got me out of that coffeehouse. Hell, you got me out of Hidden Hills. I'd still be rotting away in there, thinking Major Denver was a traitor."

"Did you think I'd let you languish at Hidden Hills and get out of our engagement? When the guy on the phone told me you didn't remember me, I thought it was a convenient way for you to get out of marrying me."

"As if I'd want to do that." He kissed her, really kissed her, for the first time since they'd reconnected, and the touch of her lips felt like coming home.

He buried his hands in her hair and deepened the kiss as they connected over the pictures of their daughter on the computer screen. He whispered against her mouth, "I love you, Paige."

She pressed her hand against his chest, one finger resting in the hollow of his throat where his pulse galloped. "I've been waiting so long to hear those words from you."

"Let's not waste any more time." He cinched her wrists lightly with his fingers. "We haven't even checked out the sleeping arrangements yet, but I'm not spending another night without you."

Digging her fingernails into his chest, she whispered, "I wasn't planning on that, either, but I need a quick shower before I crawl into bed with anyone."

He kissed her forehead. "You do that. Find us a bed and I'll make sure everything is secured down here—including that money."

"Bring the gun with you...just in case."

She slipped away from him and he drank in the photos of Ivy for several more seconds before shutting the laptop. He hauled the bag of cash into the kitchen and stuffed it into the cabinet under the sink.

He heard water running through the pipes, so Paige must've found the shower.

If he hurried, he might be able to join her. He grabbed a couple of bottles of water from the fridge and tucked them under one arm. As he flicked off the light and pivoted toward the staircase, Paige screamed.

"Asher, they're watching us."

Chapter Twelve

Asher charged into the dark bedroom, and Paige shouted, "Leave the lights."

His forward motion propelled him onward and had him tripping over a piece of furniture, banging his shin on something hard. "What the hell, Paige? I nearly killed myself getting here. Who's watching us?"

Turning back to the window, Paige hooked her finger on one of the slats of the blinds. "There's someone out there on the boat dock, and he has a pair of binoculars trained on the house."

Asher's adrenaline flared and then receded. He caught his breath. "Did he see you?"

"I don't think so, not from this window, but he must've seen the light from the bathroom." She adjusted the towel around her body with one hand, causing it to slip farther off her chest. "I came in here from my shower, and on my way to the light switch by the bed, I stopped to peer out this window. I figured the house had a view of the bay. I saw the bay, all right, but I also caught a glimpse of something shiny by the boat dock. It was a figure, a man, turned toward the house and holding something to his face—I'm sure they're binoculars."

"He's still there?"

"Yes. Is it possible we were followed?"

"Anything's possible, but if he were after us and knew we were here, why's he waiting outside in plain view? And if he were following us, how did he get here before we did?"

Paige let the slat drop. "That makes sense, but what doesn't make sense is that guy spying on the house from the boat dock."

"It's not surprising. If a soldier is on the run, who's he going to contact for help?"

"The members of his unit, but this isn't even Cam's house."

"Because Cam's house is nowhere near this area."

"I guess everyone, including the bad guys, knew about Cam's new girlfriend except us."

Keeping away from the window, Asher perched on the edge of the bed and rubbed his shin. "Is your phone up here? I'm going to give Martha a call. Cam told you to call her when we got here anyway, right?"

Paige stepped away from the window, her back still rigid, fear still etched on her face. She yanked her sweater off the chair and dipped her hand in its pocket. "It's here, and I have Martha's number programmed into it."

She handed it to him, and he slid off the mattress to the floor. "We don't want to show any more light in here than we have to."

He tapped the phone for Martha's number and held his breath through two rings.

A soft voice answered. "Hello?"

"Martha, this is Asher Knight, Cam's friend." He put the phone on speaker and nodded to Paige.

"Y-yes. I recognized the phone number Cam gave me. Did you get to the house okay? Is it stocked with food? Is the money there? I arranged everything, and my mother won't be home for another few months. A doctor should be showing up tomorrow—unless you need him right now."

"No. Everything's fine…except there's a man watching the house with binoculars from the boat dock."

She gasped. "Cam was worried someone might be watching him…us. This conspiracy is so deep and wide, I still don't feel safe."

"You don't?" Asher raised his brows at Paige, sitting on the floor next to him, and she shrugged her shoulders.

Martha said, "I'm the one who received the fake emails implicating Major Denver. Cam and I even proved the emails were phony, but it didn't stop the locomotive that's barreling forward to nail Denver for treason."

"This is messed up." Asher ran a hand over his mouth. "So the guy watching your house now may just be trying to get lucky on the chance that Cam is helping me."

"That could be it, unless you think someone followed you or tracked you. I have an idea. My mother has a cleaning lady who comes by the house all the time. She's the one who laid in the food supplies. If she were at the house now and noticed someone watching it, she'd call the police."

"Martha, this is Paige. You want us to call the police?"

Martha answered, "I'll do it and pretend I'm her. The cops will go out there to investigate and chase the guy off, and maybe he'll believe the only person at the house is my mother's cleaning lady. He wouldn't figure you two would call the cops…unless he already saw you."

Asher glanced at Paige and she shook her head. "Not that we know of, but if the police chase him off, he'll be back and I'll lose an opportunity to get my hands on someone who could give me some answers."

"Get your hands on him?" Paige's eyes widened in her pale face. "I don't think that's a good idea."

"I think it's a great idea." Asher smacked a hand on the floor. "Martha, is there a way I can get from the house to the boat dock without being seen by someone down by the water?"

Paige poked his leg, but he ignored her.

"You can get down to the water from a path next to the house. He won't see you coming that way—until you reach the bay. He's going to see you once you start approaching him from the shoreline."

"Unless I come up from the water."

Martha responded, "He'll hear a boat coming, even if it's a rowboat."

"I'm not talking about hitting the water in a boat."

Both women gasped at the same time—in stereo.

Paige jabbed his leg again. "You are *not* going into that water and swimming up on some guy who probably has a gun."

Martha joined in as soon as Paige left off. "The bay will be freezing cold."

"I won't be in there long…and Paige can warm me up once I'm back inside."

"Not if you're dead." Paige scowled at him.

Martha sighed. "If I've learned anything about you D-Boys after hanging out with Cam these past few months, I know you can't be dissuaded once you've made up your minds."

"You'd think my fiancée would know that by now, too." He ran a hand down Paige's leg.

"Then that's the way to go. Slip out the side door and duck through the fence on that side of the property. Take the path straight to the waterline and slip in from there. You'll know when you're at our dock because of the pilings in the water. I know Cam will be disappointed he wasn't there to help you."

"He helped us plenty. And tell that hothead to keep being a hothead. He should talk it up about how I'm a…traitorous bastard. I think those were his original words. If the agents behind this setup believe Cam still thinks I'm accusing Denver of sabotage, maybe they'll leave him—and you—alone."

"I'll tell him when I can. Be careful… These people will stop at nothing to keep spinning the lie about Major Denver, and we don't know why or who's behind it."

"We'll watch our backs."

Asher ended the call and crawled to the window. "I'd better make sure he's still there and not on the porch instead."

Paige blew out a breath. "This is bigger than we thought. Bigger than a few doctors at Hidden Hills."

"I always thought it was. I'm just sorry you're involved."

"I was always going to be involved, Asher." She scooted on the floor and joined him under the window. "Let me look. I can keep watch while you're on your way. If he makes a move toward the house, I'll start turning on all the lights. That'll be our signal."

"Okay. I'll keep an eye on the house on my way to the water. If I see the lights go on, I'll head back." He gestured toward the gun. "You keep that with you here. I can't take it in the water anyway."

She lifted the bottom of the blinds. "He's still there. You know, if they're watching Cam and his girlfriend, they would've been watching me."

"Probably." He crawled to the bedroom door. "Stay here. With any luck, I'll be bringing our prey back with me."

Putting one hand over her heart, she nodded. "I'll be ready. Be careful and don't do anything stupid."

"I think those two might be mutually exclusive."

Paige blew him a kiss from her position under the window. "I'd give you a real one, but I don't want to give that guy out there a target."

"I don't think he can see us behind the blinds in a dark room—" he reached out as if to snatch her kiss from the air "—but I'll take this one to be on the safe side."

Asher jogged down the stairs and exited the side door of the house. Staying in the shadows, he hopped the fence that separated the property from the public path to the beach and his boots crunched against the sandy dirt. He'd have to lose the boots before he entered the water unless he wanted to sink to the bottom of the bay.

He hunched forward and made a beeline to the water's edge, occasionally casting a glance over his shoulder at the house to watch for the signal. The house remained in darkness.

About ten feet from the shore, he dashed for a small boathouse with the stranger on the other side. He shed his jacket and pulled off his boots. On his hands and knees he made his way to the water's edge, the rocks biting into his kneecaps and palms.

He held his breath and rolled into the frigid bay, his insides curling up as the water embraced him, soaking into his clothing and his flesh.

He swam beneath the surface, frog-kicking his legs, keeping his left hand outstretched to feel for the pilings of the boat dock. When he reached the other side, he rose to the surface, tipping his head back to take a sip of air.

With his face out of the water, he paddled around to face Martha's house. The stranger had his back to the bay, silently watching the house. His power-boat bobbed in the water and Asher used it for additional cover.

Asher didn't have any room for error. If the man heard him coming out of the water and he took too long to get out, he'd probably wind up with a bullet in the head and this bay would be his watery grave.

He floated to the edge of the dock. In one movement, he hoisted himself out of the water and launched at the man.

The cover of darkness, the element of surprise and the fact that the man had both hands on his binoculars all worked in Asher's favor.

Before the stranger could react, Asher had tackled him and smashed his face against the binoculars.

The man grunted and struggled beneath him, trying to free his right hand pinned between his body and Asher's knee. Asher helped him out and shoved his hand into the pocket the man was trying to reach.

His fingers curled around the handle of a gun and he whipped it out and pressed it against the man's temple. "Who the hell are you and why are you watching the house?"

The man grunted and swore. His body bucked beneath Asher's.

"It's not gonna go that way. You're gonna answer my questions, or you're a dead man."

The man narrowed his eyes and spit out of the side of his mouth.

"Your stubbornness is gonna get you killed." Asher pushed off the man's body and rose above him, aiming the gun at his chest. "Get up."

The man staggered to his feet, the binoculars swinging from his neck.

Asher ripped them off and kicked the back of the man's legs. "Get moving—toward the house. If you try anything, I'll shoot."

They walked in silence, one ahead of the other, the swishing, sloshing sounds of Asher's wet clothing the only noise.

As they approached the back door, the patio lights illuminated their way. Then the door swung open and Paige greeted them with Asher's weapon pointed at them.

"You did it."

"I surprised him. He hasn't said a word yet…but he will."

Asher prodded the man into the house as Paige slammed the back door behind them. She scooted past Asher and his prisoner and settled a dining room chair on the hardwood floor. "Have him sit here. I found rope and tape in the garage."

Asher searched the man's pockets and pulled out a phone and a set of keys. Placing a hand on the man's shoulder, he shoved him into the chair. As Paige held her gun on their captive, Asher tied the man's ankles to the legs of the chair and secured his hands behind him.

"Let's start over." He put his face close to the other man's. "Who the hell are you and why are you watching this house?"

The captive licked his lips. "Why are you doing this? Why didn't you just call the police?"

Asher kicked the leg of the chair and the man's

head snapped back and forth. "I'm asking the questions. What are you doing here?"

"I'm casing the place." He lifted his narrow shoulders. "This is a ritzy neighborhood and I heard this house was empty."

"Then why are you out there watching it instead of breaking in?"

"Wanted to make sure it was empty. I came by boat, saw a light go on upstairs, and that stopped me."

"Stopped you, so why didn't you go away? Find another house to burglarize?"

"This is the one I was told to hit."

Paige jerked her head toward Asher. "*Told* to hit? Someone commissioned you to burglarize this property?"

"Not like that." The man shook his head back and forth, the ends of his scraggly hair spewing droplets of water from Asher's watery takedown. "Just heard a rumor around town about some of these fancy beach houses and the ones left vacant. This was one of them."

"That still makes no sense. I don't know many thieves who would stay back from a property they wanted to break into and watch it with binoculars."

The man snorted. "You know many thieves?"

Asher growled. "You have no idea."

"Are you acting alone in this plan?" Paige still held the gun, but she'd let it slip from her tight grip. "Is there anyone else out there?"

The man's dark eyes flickered. "Just me."

"I don't believe you." Asher's jaw ached from tension and shivering. How the hell was he going to get information out of this guy…especially with Paige here watching?

"Believe it or not, buddy. Why aren't you calling the police? Did you two break in here, too?" He laughed, and the laugh turned into a hacking cough.

"And what if we did? What would the police discover about you? Some nobody who doesn't exist anywhere? A fake ID? Fingerprints leading to no one?"

A muscle twitched in the corner of the man's eye.

He knew something. Asher lunged at him and closed his hand around his throat until the man's eyes bulged from the sockets. "Tell me who you work for and what you were doing outside this house."

The man choked and his body squirmed in the chair.

Asher released him suddenly, and the chair tipped on its back legs. "Answer me."

Asher felt Paige's hand on his back, and his spine stiffened. He couldn't properly question the man with Paige looking on in judgment.

The man's eyes watered and one tear slipped from the corner of his left eye. "Go to hell."

Gritting his teeth, Asher stalked to the kitchen and pulled a knife from a block on the counter. He returned to his prisoner, avoiding Paige's wide-eyed stare.

He loomed over the man, wielding the knife at

his throat. "You're going to tell me what I want to know, starting now."

The man's Adam's apple bobbed as he swallowed, but he pressed his lips together and closed his eyes. "I already told ya."

Asher flicked the blade against the man's flesh, and a drop of blood beaded on the side of his neck. "You can die from a thousand paper cuts just as assuredly as you can from a slice across your jugular."

Paige sucked in a breath behind him.

"Take your best shot, buddy."

Asher tapped Paige's right arm, the gun dangling from her fingers. "Keep your weapon trained on him. I'll be right back."

Asher strode to the door leading to the garage and flipped on the light. He scanned the tool bench against the wall, noting the drawers Paige had left open in her search for rope, and slid a hammer and a pair of pliers from the hooks on the wall.

He returned to the dining room, untied the man's hands and grabbed one, splaying his fingers on the arm of the chair.

"Hey, hey, hey." The man tried to snatch his hand back, but Asher drove his fist into the back of his hand.

Then he brought the hammer down on one of the man's fingers and the guy let out a howl, which blended with Paige's cry.

"Why are you here and on whose orders?"

The man's mouth twisted. "You think you can do anything worse to me than they can?"

Asher's heart skipped a beat. "Now we're getting somewhere. Who's they? Who sent you to watch this house and why?"

The man curled his good fingers into the arm of the chair. "You already know why I was sent here. I was told to watch this house, the house of Cam Sutton's girlfriend, to keep an eye out for you."

"Why? What are they trying to do to Asher?" Paige squared herself in front of the man, crossing her arms over her chest.

Asher raised the hammer again—this time over the man's kneecap.

His leg bounced. "I—I think you know that already, too. They want him to implicate Major Rex Denver. They want him to report that it was Denver who killed that ranger and Denver who pushed him over the cliff."

"He's right, Paige." Asher lowered the hammer but kept a firm grip on it. "We already know why they're after us and what they want me to do. The question is, who's behind all this? Who's behind the setup of Major Denver and why?"

"That I don't know." The man hunched his shoulders. "But it's big."

"I-is anyone else coming here? Did you contact your backups?"

"I haven't contacted anyone. I saw a light on in the house and started watching. I didn't know if it was Martha Drake back in the house or her mother or the cleaning lady."

They already knew a lot about Martha. Asher

pointed to the phone he'd dropped on the floor. "Check it out, Paige."

She swept the phone up from the floor. "Password?"

The man dropped his chin to his chest.

Asher nudged his shoe with his bare foot and held up the pliers in his other hand. "You know I'll use them. The way I was treated in Hidden Hills? Made me kinda crazy."

Paige nodded beside him and held up the phone. "Give me your password. There's nothing I can do to stop him."

The man licked his lips and reeled off a four-digit code.

Paige entered the password and the phone came to life. "His name's Peter. Last text was from an hour ago—about the time I spotted him outside. Just says 'lights on in the house.'"

"Who'd he text?"

"A contact named Linc."

"Who's Linc?" Asher kicked the chair leg.

The man's head snapped up. "He's my guy. The one who gives me orders. The one I report to."

"Any calls, Paige?"

"An incoming call a few hours ago, just a number, no contact name."

"What is this organization? Who are you working for?"

"I dunno, buddy. I just do what I'm told."

"You're lying. If you were some grunt, you

wouldn't know about Major Denver and our failed meeting with his contact."

"I'm the muscle, nothing more, but it doesn't mean I don't ask questions."

Asher tipped his head toward Paige. "Text Linc back and let him know it was a false alarm—nobody at the house."

The man in the chair gurgled. "If they ever find out about this, I'm a dead man and they'd have more than hammers and pliers to use."

"Sounds like a highly organized group, a group that doesn't fool around. Is it linked to the US government? It has to be with the personnel installed at Hidden Hills. What names have you heard? What else has Linc told you?"

"I don't know. I can't think." He bucked in the chair. "I have to use the bathroom. Just give me a break here, man. I don't have any more weapons on me. I'm cooperating, right?"

Paige nudged Asher's back.

Trading the tools for a gun, Asher said, "I'll let you get up and use the bathroom, but I'm coming with you. If you try anything, I'll shoot you."

While Asher held the man at gunpoint, Paige untied his ankles.

The man rose to his feet slowly, rubbing his forearms beneath the long sleeves of his shirt.

"Move." Asher waved the gun toward the half bathroom next to the garage door.

The man took a tentative step forward and covered his mouth with one hand.

"I thought you were desperate to use the head. Get going before I decide this is a ploy and shoot you."

The man took another stumbling step and then dropped to his knees.

Paige gasped. "Is he going for a weapon?"

Asher aimed a kick at the man's back and he pitched forward, his head turning to the side.

"Shoot him, Asher. Stop him."

Asher crouched down, rolling him to his side. The man's eyes bugged out and his tongue protruded from his mouth. Asher rested two fingers against his pulse.

"I don't have to shoot him, Paige. He's dead."

Chapter Thirteen

Paige gripped the handle of the gun, still pointing it at the man's head. When he'd dropped to his knees, adrenaline had flooded her body and it still coursed through her.

"H-how? How is he dead?" She stared at the man's slack mouth and bugged-out eyes.

"I'm not sure, but I think he took something. He was reaching into his sleeves when he got up. He covered his mouth."

Her own mouth dropped open. "He poisoned himself?"

"It looks like it." He pointed to the tongue, now turning bright red.

"He committed suicide rather than tell us any more about this organization."

"He must've had orders to do so. Once his bosses found out he'd been compromised, lost his phone, gave up his phone's password—they probably had a little homecoming planned for him that would make a few broken fingers look like child's play."

She'd been afraid when Asher had dragged this

man back to the house. She hadn't wanted to watch as he brought the hammer down on his hand, and she didn't want to think about where this would all lead.

She swallowed. "Would you have let him go?"

"I don't know." Asher swiped a bead of water from his forehead.

"What are we going to do with his body now?"

"Bring it back to the water. He has a boat at the dock. That's how he got here. We can leave him in the boathouse. Nobody's going to find him there at this time of year."

Paige shivered. "Leave him for Martha's mother to discover?"

"She's not due back for a while. We'll let his co-horts know the location of his body later, and they can pick him up. They're not going to allow the death of one of their own to be investigated by a local PD."

Crossing her arms, Paige cupped her elbows with her hands. "Do you think we're safe here?"

"No."

"We're going to have to hit the road again, aren't we?"

"At least we have a bundle of cash now."

"The doctor. You need to see the doctor, Asher. I can't have you collapsing on me again."

"We'll stay here for what's left of the night and get him out here tomorrow morning. Then we leave."

Paige glanced at the dead man's phone on the dining room table. "Linc hasn't responded yet, but maybe we can convince him that this house is a dead end."

"At some point his bosses are going to have another assignment for this guy." Asher nudged the man's foot. "What's going to happen when he doesn't show up? Doesn't respond?"

"We can pretend to be Peter for a little while. It could buy us some time in this house."

"We'll see." Asher crouched next to the dead man. "I'm gonna get him out of here first."

"I'll help you."

"You sure?" Asher raised his brows.

"He's my problem, too. In fact, I probably want him out of here more than you do." She spun toward the kitchen. "I am going to get a pair of gloves first."

"At least there's no blood to clean up."

Paige stuck her head in the cupboard beneath the kitchen sink and found a pair of rubber gloves. She pulled them on and joined Asher, who'd already heaved the man's body over his shoulder.

"Get the doors, clear a path for me and use the light from the cell phone to guide us."

Paige scurried ahead of Asher lugging the body of a dead man and opened the back door. She led him down to the boat dock and swung open the door to the boathouse.

"There's a light. Should I turn it on?"

"No. You never know who might be watching out here."

Paige flicked the little beam of light around the boathouse. "Let's wrap him in this piece of canvas. It's big enough, probably meant for a boat."

"Good idea. Spread it out." Asher stepped into the boathouse, panting in the small, close place.

Paige unrolled the canvas. As Asher ducked and started to slide the man off his shoulder, Paige grabbed lifeless arms dangling to the floor.

Together, they heaved him into the middle of the canvas.

Asher stepped back and brushed his hands together. "That's some kind of devotion to off yourself for the cause—whatever that cause is."

"Maybe he didn't do it for the cause. Maybe he did it out of fear of what they'd do to him after getting caught."

"Either way, it's extreme."

Paige studied Asher's profile in the dim light. "Would you do it? If the enemy captured you, would you kill yourself rather than give up information?"

"I'd suffer torture rather than give up intel. But call me an optimist, I'd never give up hope that I'd be rescued." His jawline hardened to granite. "That's why we can't give up on Denver."

For the next ten minutes, they busied themselves with rolling up the body in the sheet of canvas and shoving it to the back of the boathouse.

Paige puffed out a breath. "I really hope nobody finds his body before his associates come and collect him. This looks more like a murder than a suicide, and we've probably implicated ourselves in a hundred ways in that house."

"That's why it's best we leave him in here instead of dumping him in the water. We don't want him washing up on the shore somewhere, and nobody's going to come out here in the dead of winter. The house is isolated enough that no neighbors are going to be reporting a foul odor."

Paige wrinkled her nose. "Let's go back to the house and clean up there just in case."

"I'm anxious to see if Linc has responded yet. In fact, I'm looking forward to playing a few games with Linc. He's our best lead yet."

They took the public beach path back to the house, and Asher picked up his boots and jacket. When they got back, they wiped down the hammer, the pliers and all the tools they'd used to subjugate their intruder and put them away.

Then Paige turned to Asher and plucked at his damp shirt. "You need to take a warm shower. I'll dump these clothes in the washing machine."

While Asher undid the top two buttons of his flannel, the cell phone on the dining room table buzzed. He lunged for it and held it up. "The password?"

She gave him the four numbers and he tapped the phone.

"It's Linc. 'Confirm position.'"

"How are you going to respond?"

He spoke aloud as he typed the text. "'Still at house, no movement.'"

Paige put a hand over her mouth as she waited.

Five seconds later, Asher read, "'Roger. Keep watching.'"

"There. That's a sign that you can take a shower and we can get some rest. Nobody followed us here.

Nobody knows we're here except Cam and Martha. The dead man in the boathouse was assigned to watch this house just in case."

"I could use a shower and some dry clothes, but I'll feel a lot better if you keep that gun in your hand and keep watch."

"As much as I'd rather be in that shower with you, I'm on it."

He undid the rest of his buttons and sloughed off the shirt. As he handed it to her, he grabbed her hand. "Paige, you continue to amaze me with your strength. I couldn't ask for a better partner."

She brought his hand to her lips and pressed them against his knuckles. "Ditto for me. You've always been my strength, Asher. It comes off you in waves and I just soak it up free."

He slipped away from her and charged upstairs, calling over his shoulder, "I won't be long. Stay vigilant."

Paige peeked out the front window, but nothing stirred out there. Nobody in this little wealthy enclave had a clue that they'd stashed a dead body in the boathouse.

She crept upstairs and through the bedroom to the bathroom, filled with steam. She could still make out Asher's naked body behind the glass shower door.

"Just here to get the rest of your wet clothes."

He opened the shower door and sluiced a hand across his wet hair. "All quiet out there?"

"Uh-huh." Her gaze dropped from his face and skimmed down his body.

"When you look at me like that, it makes me wanna pull you in here with me."

"I would take you up on it, but—" she pulled the gun from the back of her waistband "—vigilance."

"Yeah, just don't wave that thing around in here… or any lower."

She swept his clothes from the top of the toilet seat, where he'd piled them up, and tucked them under her arm. "I'll take care of these. Then maybe we can get a little shut-eye before we start the day."

He'd ducked back under the water and didn't seem to have heard her.

Sighing, she trudged down the stairs. If the man with the binoculars hadn't been spying on them, she and Asher might be tucked into bed together right now…and that man would still be alive and maybe getting ready to break in.

She stuffed the clothes in the washing machine and checked for a message from Linc when she reached the kitchen. Nothing. At this time of the morning, he must be sleeping. He must be convinced Peter hadn't seen anyone at Martha's house. How long could they keep up the ruse?

She used the charger from her old phone to plug in Peter's phone to keep it juiced up. They didn't want to lose connection with Linc.

She left her phone turned off. She'd already called Terrence to let him know they'd found another source of money.

While the teakettle whistled, Asher poked his head into the kitchen.

"Tea?"

"No, thanks." He stepped out, fanning a blanket around his shoulders. "No pajamas, but I feel one hundred percent better after that warm shower."

She poured the boiling water on the tea bag in the cup. "Do you think we can get a little sleep?"

"Sure, so why are you drinking that tea?"

"It's herbal." She flicked the tag hanging over the edge of the cup. "It's just for warmth and comfort."

"I guess I haven't been much good for warmth and comfort." He spread out his arms, opening the blanket. "Come here."

She moved toward him like a magnet and stopped inches from his body.

He enfolded her in his arms, wrapping the blanket around her. He kissed the top of her head. "You need some sleep. I'll keep watch."

"We'll both keep watch. If you can't sleep, I'll stay awake for support."

"I can sleep in the car or at our next stop—provided that one's not compromised like this one."

She wriggled free from the cocoon of his embrace. "I'll drink my tea to stay awake."

"You just said it was herbal." He strolled to the sofa and sat down in one corner.

"It is, but it'll keep me occupied." She dropped the tea bag into the trash and cupped the mug with both hands. Then she joined Asher on the sofa, curling her legs beneath her.

He draped his arm and one edge of the blanket around her shoulders.

She took a sip of her warm brew and rested her head on Asher's shoulder. "I can't wait to go home and see Ivy. She'll be so excited to have her daddy home."

"It's gonna happen, Paige. We'll all be together, safe." He stroked her hair, and she closed her eyes.

The cup felt heavy in her hands, and she must've communicated this to Asher, because he took it from her. She didn't even make an attempt to hold on to it.

Her eyelids grew as heavy as the cup had been, and she struggled to open them, but Asher's warm touch continued down the side of her neck and shoulder, caressing her, soothing her as only he could.

As she drifted off to sleep, she had one last surge of energy and she blinked her eyes. She mumbled, "I'm supposed to be taking care of you."

"Shh, it's my turn now."

And for the first time, she felt worthy of his protection.

THE SMELL OF bacon tickled her nose, and for a few seconds Paige imagined she was at her mom's house with Ivy. Then she peeled open her eyes, took in the room with its lavish decor, and reality hit her smack between the eyes.

She sat up on the sofa, and the blanket slipped from her shoulders. "Asher?"

"I'm in the kitchen, making breakfast. You were sleeping so soundly—" he hunched over the counter "—I didn't want to disturb you. Good news."

"The guy in the boathouse is still dead and no-body has found him yet?"

"Yeah, that, too." He held up one of the phones charging on the counter. "Linc has agreed to a meeting."

Paige blinked. "What? Agreed to whose meeting?"

"Our meeting?"

"You set up a meeting with Linc?"

"How else am I going to start working my way up the chain of command to get to the top dog?"

"When and where is this meeting taking place?"

"Don't have all the details yet. Maybe we'll meet him right here." He held up a plate of bacon. "We have everything we need for now."

"I don't know." Paige scooted off the sofa and stretched. "You shouldn't have let me fall asleep. I'll bet you didn't get any."

"I'll sleep later. Who knows? Maybe blacking out like that stored up my energy."

"Which reminds me." She snapped her fingers. "We need to call Martha's friend this morning—the doctor. What if you pass out before our meeting with Linc?"

"Not optimal." He pinched a piece of bacon between his fingers and bit off the end. "Pretty good. I made eggs, too."

She pulled a stool up to the counter and straddled it. "I see you dried your clothes and got dressed. How long have you been up?"

"Just over an hour."

"Nobody snooping around the boathouse?"

"I don't think we have to worry about that, Paige. The boathouse is on private property. Nobody has any reason to suspect anything. Even Linc doesn't know Peter's current condition."

She pulled Peter's phone toward her by the cord, entered his password and read the text exchange between Linc and Asher. "So, he made contact first?"

"Asked for an update. As you can read, I told him no movement and inquired about our next move."

"How's this going to work?" She nodded as Asher held a spatula full of scrambled eggs over a plate.

"Not sure yet. Maybe an ambush."

"With all your busy texting, did you contact the doc yet?"

"No. Do you want to do the honors?"

"He needs to get here before Linc does if we're meeting him at this house." She wrinkled her nose. "And if we are, that boathouse is going to get pretty crowded."

"As long as we're not among its inhabitants." He winked and dumped the eggs onto her plate.

An hour later, Martha's friend knocked at the door. As Paige put her eye to the peephole, the doctor took a step back and displayed his hospital ID with his name printed on it.

Grabbing the handle of the door, she glanced at Asher hovering to her right, his gun drawn. "He's legit."

Asher pocketed his gun, and Paige swung open the door with a smile. "Dr. Tucker? Thanks for coming out."

"Call me Preston. Martha and I go way back to our prep school days, and I'd do anything for her."

"Can I get you something to drink?"

"Something hot. It's getting cold out there." Preston clamped his black bag between his body and arm and rubbed his hands together.

"Hot tea?" She jerked her thumb at Asher. "He's the patient. Asher, Preston."

As the two men shook hands, Asher said, "I don't know how much Martha told you…"

Preston held up one hand. "I don't need to know the how or why. Martha explained your issue to me, and I believe I have a remedy. I'm going to need to take some of your blood, and I'm going to give you a shot as a counteragent if it's what I think it is. If after looking at your blood, it turns out to be something else, I'll let you know."

Asher narrowed his eyes. "If it's not what you think it is and you give me the shot anyway, is that going to have some negative effect on me? Kill me? Make me impotent?"

Paige snorted.

Preston shoved his glasses up the bridge of his nose, all business. "If it's not the drug I believe to be running through your system, this antidote is harmless. If I analyze your blood and find something else…I'll have to do more research."

"And he'll continue to be affected." Paige laced her fingers in front of her and squeezed them together to keep from fidgeting nervously.

"He may continue to pass out at random intervals." Preston's thin lips eked out a smile. "But let's think positive thoughts."

His head flicked from side to side like a bird's. "Can we sit at the dining room table?"

Paige retrieved a clean dish towel from beneath the sink and spread it on the table. As Preston readied his tools of the trade, Paige put on the teakettle.

"Asher, do you want some water?"

"Yeah, thanks." He looked up from rolling the sleeve of his shirt and exposing his veins for Preston.

She placed a glass of water on the table next to Asher as Preston swiped an antiseptic pad over the inside of his elbow. "Your tea is coming up."

Preston nodded and then held up a vial between two fingers. "I'm not going to take much. Just enough to fill this vial."

Paige turned away as the needle plunged into Asher's arm. The teakettle's whistle saved her and she scurried to the kitchen, anxious to get away from the sight of Asher's blood pumping into the glass container.

She prepped the tea and returned to the dining room table, carrying a mug in each hand. "Good, I missed the gory stuff."

Asher raised his brows at her and her cheeks warmed. Of course, they'd just hauled a body from the house, but Peter hadn't been bleeding anywhere, which made rolling him up in canvas a lot less icky than seeing blood trickle down the side of a glass vial.

Setting the mug in front of Preston, she asked, "Milk or sugar?"

"Black is fine." Preston capped the vial and slipped it into a plastic bag. "One more needle, if you can take it."

"I have to admit, I've had my fill of needles, but if this is the last one, I can take it." Asher presented his other arm. "How's it going to make me feel? Any immediate reaction?"

"It might feel like you just drank five energy drinks, but that will subside." He tapped the water glass with the needle. "Keep drinking water."

"And if I still pass out today like I did yesterday?"

"It means my diagnosis and assessment were wrong, and you should call me immediately."

Paige took her tea and wandered to the back door, staring out at the boat dock. They hadn't done anything wrong. Peter had killed himself. They couldn't have saved him even if they'd called 911.

She pressed the warm cup against her face. Second house, second dead body. Would Linc be a third? What would Asher have done with Peter if he hadn't offed himself? What would he do with Linc if he didn't get the answers he wanted?

"All done, chicken."

She glanced over her shoulder. "I don't mind injections, but I don't like the blood."

"I'm finished." Preston peeled the gloves from his hands. "I'm confident we did the right thing here."

"What do we owe you?" Asher gulped down the rest of his water and pushed back from the table.

"Nothing. If you're a friend of Martha's, you're a friend of mine." Preston cupped the mug in his hands and slurped a sip of tea. "You're military, like Martha's new guy?"

"Yeah."

Preston squinted at Asher through the steam rising from his tea. "That's it. Don't look so fierce. I'm not going to interrogate you. I told you I didn't need the details."

Paige studied Preston's face. Had he been crushing on Martha before that big, tough D-Boy Cam Sutton had come in and swept her off her feet? "Did you have a thing for Martha?"

"Me?" One side of Preston's mouth turned up as he took off his glasses and wiped them with a cloth. "She's a darling girl, but I'm gay. That's how we got close in school—just a couple of misfits in that environment."

"We appreciate your help, Preston." Asher pressed a hand against his chest. "You weren't kidding about the adrenaline rush."

"Are you okay?" Preston reached for his bag. "I can take your blood pressure."

"I'm okay." Asher held up his water glass. "I'll keep drinking this stuff, right?"

"It'll pass within an hour or so. You can reach me at the number you called before if you need help. If that blood test doesn't yield the result I expect, I'll be calling you." Preston took a few more sips of his tea. "Is that all you need?"

"What else do you have in that black bag?" Asher leveled an unsteady finger at Preston's medical bag on the table.

"A full complement of medical supplies…and some drugs. What is it you're looking for, Asher?"

Paige's eyes popped open as she watched Asher pace to the window and back. Had he become dependent on those drugs he'd been getting at Hidden Hills? She wouldn't put it past that bunch to get Asher addicted.

"If you have it, I'd like a syringe or two of something that can knock someone out—fast, put 'em out like—" Asher snapped his fingers "—that."

"No lasting effects but fast-acting and total?"

"That's it."

"I have just the thing." Preston unzipped his bag and plucked two plastic wrapped syringes from an inside pocket. He smacked them down on the table. "The effects of this should last a good twenty-four hours. Best administered in a large muscle, like a thigh or buttocks."

"Through clothing?" Asher returned to the table and nudged the needles with his finger.

"As long as the needle goes through." Preston drained his teacup and clicked it back onto the table. "Now, before I let my feelings for Martha get me into any more trouble, I'll leave you."

Paige handed Preston his coat at the door. "Thank you so much, Preston."

"Thanks, man." Asher thrust out his hand. "And remember, discretion."

"Do you think I want anything I've done today to get out? I'm asking for the same."

"We never heard of you."

When they sent Preston on his way, Paige spun toward Asher. "What are you going to use those for?"

"Might come in handy for Linc or anyone else who decides to make a move on us."

She placed both hands on his shoulders. "How are you feeling? Still hyped up?"

"Yeah. Maybe I should take a jog along the bay to work it off."

"Don't you dare. We don't want anyone to spot us here. If the police find Peter's body before his associates do, we could be investigated for murder. Fingerprints, fiber—Homicide would have a field day with all the evidence."

"But we didn't kill Peter. He killed himself." Asher wrenched away from her to take a lap around the family room.

She tracked him with her gaze. "I don't know about you, but I don't even want to go down that road."

"Paige, that's the least of our worries. The people setting up Major Denver, the people after us are never going to allow one of their own to become the subject of a murder investigation or even a missing person's investigation."

She put a hand to her head. "I'm getting anxious just watching you. Are you sure you're okay? Can you sit down for a minute?"

"I'm fine—agitated, just like the doc warned."

"I don't want to have that meeting with Linc until you're…unagitated. There's no telling what you'll do to him in this state."

"Preston said this will last just about an hour. We have plenty of time. I'd rather get Linc out here in the cover of darkness."

"How are we going to spend the rest of the afternoon?"

"Oh, I don't know. Our enemies are off our trail for the time being, it's cold outside and warm inside, and I'm hopped up on something that's giving me an incredible sense of vitality." He wiggled his eyebrows up and down. "I can think of the perfect way to spend an afternoon alone with my fiancée."

"I don't know if I'll be able to keep up with the Energizer Bunny." Paige tilted her head and pursed her lips, but her heart had started racing.

"There's only one way to find out." He swooped in and swept her off her feet.

She screamed and kicked her legs, a sense of relief flooding her body with the thought that maybe they could find some normalcy in this unnatural situation.

Asher stooped next to the coffee table and her legs dipped down as he grabbed his gun. "I hope this doesn't kill the romance for you."

"The fact that you want to keep me safe only heightens it." She tucked her head in the crook of his neck. So much for normalcy.

Asher carried her up the stairs effortlessly and eagerly. Either he couldn't wait to make love or his current manic state was driving him.

One way or the other, she didn't care. Instead she squealed when he kicked open the bedroom door.

He dumped her on the bed and she scrambled to

her knees, tugging on the hem of Asher's T-shirt. "You've been teasing me with this bod for days now—playing peek-a-boo with your backside in the hospital gown, taking showers with your clothes off."

"Imagine that." He spread his arms so she could roll his shirt up his torso.

"Go ahead and pull it off. I can't reach that high."

He yanked the shirt over his head and tossed it over his shoulder.

Paige skimmed her hands over his chest and hooked her fingers in the waistband of his jeans. "I knew there was a good reason why I didn't buy you a belt."

He tapped his foot while she undid the buttons of his fly. "You can't move any faster than that?"

"You'd better slow down, mister. I've waited a long time for this moment, and I'm not going to be rushed."

His chest expanded as he took a big breath, and his lashes fluttered closed. "I'll try."

Paige opened his fly and peeled his jeans from his hips. She ran her hand across the front of his briefs. "Do you think that antidote is going to give you a ramped-up erection, too?"

"I think I'm already there."

Paige clicked her tongue. "I told you to slow down."

"I think daytime sex should be rowdier and faster, don't you?"

"Oh, is that the problem? It's too light out for

you?" Paige scooted off the bed. "I'm going to close these drapes and trick you."

She bounded to the window and grabbed handfuls of the drapes on either side of the window, her gaze automatically shifting to the boathouse with the dead guy inside—or so she thought.

A chill gripped the back of her neck and she choked. "My God. It's Peter."

"Someone found him?"

She whipped her head around, clutching one side of the drapes to her body. "No, he came back to life."

Chapter Fourteen

Asher pressed his face to the glass, fogging it up. He wiped a circle with his fist and swore again.

His gaze locked onto Peter, or someone who looked a lot like him, standing outside the boathouse staring at the bay.

"Maybe it's not him. Maybe it's someone else."

"Which could be almost as bad. I don't understand. Peter was dead." Paige's eyes took up half her face. "Wasn't he?"

"Let's ask him." Asher yanked up his jeans and dived across the bed to grab his T-shirt and gun. As he raced down the stairs, he heard Paige coming in fast after him. He twisted his head over his shoulder when he reached the first floor. "Stay here."

"Are you kidding? I've never seen a man come back from the dead before."

Asher pulled on his boots and struggled into his jacket as he lunged for the back door.

With his gun in his pocket, he charged across the back lawn toward the water's edge. If Peter had all his faculties, he wasn't using them.

The man gazing out at the bay didn't even turn around, didn't make a move.

Asher scooped in a deep breath and grabbed Peter from behind with one arm. Although the man in his grasp wasn't dead, his icy-cold flesh might fool a coroner.

Peter staggered forward and then twisted around, wielding a knife.

Paige screamed. "Look out."

A second later, Asher jabbed the syringe he had in his fist into Peter's thigh through the denim of his pants.

Peter dropped immediately.

Asher looked up and down the shoreline, squinting at the other houses. "God, it's broad daylight. Is there anyone out, Paige? Did anyone witness this?"

"There's nobody. Martha said the nearest house is vacant, and the other house is too far away to see anything, unless someone has binoculars trained on us—and why would they?"

"I would've liked to have questioned him some more, but he didn't give me a choice." Asher kicked the knife that had fallen from Peter's hand into the bay.

"Preston did say the stuff in the syringe would last up to twenty-four hours, didn't he?"

"Yep. That means we'll have to get out of here after we meet with Linc."

Paige pointed to Peter's inert form on the ground. "I suppose we'd better get him back into the boathouse. I still don't understand what happened. He was not breathing when we carried him out here the first time. He didn't have a pulse."

"That we noticed." Asher crouched and slid his hand beneath Peter's arms. "The mad scientists at Hidden Hills have proved themselves to be adept at concocting a variety of strange-acting drugs. It's not a stretch to think these…agents are equipped with one that simulates death."

"He's one lucky guy." Paige backed up to the boathouse door, which Peter had left standing open. "What if we had dumped his body in the bay? He would've died for real."

"I guess it was a chance he was willing to take. He probably thought we would leave him right there in the house and make our escape."

"Maybe we should have." Paige held the boathouse door open for him as he dragged Peter back inside.

He dumped him on top of the canvas. "We don't need to wrap him up. I'm surprised he didn't suffocate in there."

"You still have the other syringe, don't you?"

"It has Linc's name on it."

After they stashed Peter in the boathouse and hooked a padlock on the outside, they returned to the house.

The antidote that had been racing through his system seemed to have diluted. After the excitement of seeing a man rise from the dead, his heart rate had returned to normal and unfortunately his raging erection had subsided.

He took a quick glance at Paige, twisting her fingers in front of her and peering through the window of the back door every ten seconds. That erection would've gone to waste, anyway. Paige's anxiety had gone through the roof.

Asher approached her from behind and touched her back. She jumped.

"He's not going to make a comeback, Paige. I trust Preston and his pharmaceuticals."

"You're going to contact Linc now, aren't you?"

"Sunset is early. The sooner we get him out here, the better. Then we can hit the road. They still don't know where we are, but when two of their grunts go missing checking out Martha's mother's house, they're gonna come calling."

"Go missing?" Paige licked her lips. "What are we going to do with them, Asher? If you kill them…"

He stroked her back. "I'm not going to kill them, Paige—unless they try to kill us first. Who knows how this group after us could spin the murder of a couple of men? Instead of being accused of going AWOL, I could be accused of murder. I'm not going to chance that."

Her shoulders slumped. "Okay. That makes me feel better—not that they deserve our mercy, but I don't want to be responsible for someone's death."

"Of course not." He swept her hair from the back of her neck and pressed his lips against the top knot of her spine.

"Tabitha…"

"We weren't responsible for that. She chose to

track me down even knowing others were on my trail. She was playing a dangerous game." He let her heavy hair fall against her back. "I'm going to text Linc."

"How are we going to play this?"

"Peter's boat is still on the bay. I'll ask Linc to meet in the boathouse. After all, why would Linc think Peter has access to the house unless he broke in? And I don't think that was part of their plan."

"Okay, so we set up the meeting for the boathouse." She pivoted from the door and leaned back against it as she crossed her arms. "Then what?"

"We ambush him. I'll make sure I check his sleeves for any hidden pills so I have a chance to question him. Then we get some answers, maybe we find the next person up the ladder, someone with some authority, some knowledge."

She smoothed her hands across his chest. "When we have enough, we have to take this to someone. Your name has to be cleared."

"Major Denver's name has to be cleared." He grabbed one of her hands and kissed her wrist.

He returned to the kitchen with Paige right behind him. He entered the password for Peter's phone and tapped his messages. Nobody had sent Peter any messages since the one from Linc earlier.

Asher read his text aloud for Paige as he entered it in the phone. "'No sign of anyone at house. Meet me here at the boathouse behind the house at five.'"

They both stared at the phone for several minutes,

and then Asher shrugged and tucked it in his pocket. "He'll respond."

"I suppose we should have some lunch." Paige stood in the middle of the kitchen, hands on her hips. "There's no telling when we'll get dinner if Linc shows up at five and we have to deal with him."

"We should also plot out our next move—literally. We need to hit the road again after we see Linc, although where we go will probably depend on what he tells us."

Standing on her tiptoes, Paige reached into a cupboard and pulled down a can. She turned it toward him. "Soup?"

"Sounds good. I saw stuff for sandwiches this morning when I was whipping up breakfast. I'll get to work on those."

Fifteen minutes later, they sat down with a plate of sandwiches and two bowls of tomato soup.

Paige slid one of the cell phones charging on the counter toward her. "I never did find out Tabitha's password. We also don't even know if they found her body yet in the cabin. I'm going to check on my computer after we eat."

"I'm sure they've found a body by now—whether they've ID'd Tabitha or not is another matter." Asher blew on a spoonful of soup and slurped it up, the rich tomatoey taste filling his mouth. "I'm sure the doctors at Hidden Hills have figured it out by now."

"I wonder if she left them a note or something. Do you think she was planning to return to work after she had you safely stashed away? I'm beginning to wonder if Tabitha's the one who injected you with that timed-release drug to control you once she had you at her cabin."

"I wouldn't put it past her, and if she wanted to return to Hidden Hills, she wouldn't have clued them in that she'd aided and abetted my escape from the center." He shrugged and took a big bite of his sandwich.

While he was chewing and Paige was going on about Tabitha, the phone in his pocket vibrated. He held up a finger to get Paige to stop talking. "Peter's phone."

He pulled the phone from his pocket and dropped it on the counter as if it burned his hand.

"What's wrong?"

"It's a call from Linc, not a text." He poked at the phone, nudging it away from him.

"Damn." Paige covered her mouth with one hand. "What are we going to do?"

"Well, I'm not going to try to pass myself as Peter, if that's what you're thinking. We don't know how well these guys know each other." He brushed his hands together and took a gulp of water. "Let it ring. I'll respond with a text later."

While he finished the last sandwich, Paige put her dishes in the sink and retrieved her laptop from the living room.

"I'm going to look for a story on that cabin."

Asher slid off his stool and took the rest of the dishes to the sink to wash them.

Paige whistled behind him. "Here's one. Explosion…cabin…gas leak. Yeah, right. Body found."

"Did they identify her?" Asher grabbed a dish towel and wiped his hands as he joined Paige and hovered over her shoulder.

"No. The article says the owners are accounted for and don't know who could've been in their cabin. The authorities are wondering if the person was a trespasser or transient. God, they don't even know if the person was a man or a woman." She raised her glassy eyes to his face.

"That was an intense fire, and there's no reason for anyone to suspect Tabitha to be in that cabin."

"What was Tabitha's last name?" Paige wiggled her fingers over the laptop's keyboard.

"Crane. Tabitha Crane. What are you going to do?"

"Look her up. See if anyone has connected her to that cabin yet."

Paige clicked away on the keyboard while Asher returned to the dishes. "How long should I wait before I text Linc back?"

"Here she is. I found her on a medical professional's site. Tabitha Carly Crane, Tabby Crane. She sounds so normal on here."

"Did you expect her to list her interests as being a lovesick stalker on a professional website?"

"Maybe you're the one who drove her mad for love." Paige peered at him over the top of the computer. "You had all the girls hot for you at that party…and you wound up with the most unstable one of all."

"I didn't see you that way, Paige. You were hurting. Anyone with half a brain could figure that out." He clenched his fists in the soapy water. Why did she have to keep dismissing herself?

She had wanted to keep him in the dark because she didn't want to relive *his* reaction to remembering his fiancée had been a drunk he didn't trust with their baby. She'd kept the truth from him because she knew she'd have to pick up that role again—constantly downgrading herself before he could do it.

"Lots of people figured out I was hurting, but nobody wanted to deal with it—except my other wild friends who had their own addictions. And we dealt with it in our own way."

"And now that part of your life is over and we have a beautiful daughter together. Let's make sure we both get home to her safely."

She rubbed one eye and pushed the laptop away from her. "What excuse are you going to give Linc for not picking up the phone?"

"I'm in the middle of nowhere, camped out in a boathouse on the shore of the bay—the reception is bad." He dried and stacked the dishes and then dug the phone from his pocket. "I think it's about time. It's almost two thirty."

Asher straddled the stool, cupping Peter's phone in one hand. "How does this sound? 'Missed your call. Reception bad on the bay. Meet at five?'"

She tipped her chin to her chest. "Go for it."

Asher entered the text and this time they didn't have to wait long. Linc responded almost immediately, as if he were waiting for Peter's communication.

"What does it say?" Paige tugged on his sleeve, leaning against his body.

"'See you at five.'"

"Great." Paige turned and looked at the room. "We should get packed up in case we need to make a quick getaway."

"Is there any other kind?"

They spent the next hour washing and packing their clothes, loading the trunk of the car with non-perishable food and stashing the bag of cash next to the food. They cleaned up the kitchen, stripped the sheets of the bed for the housekeeper and got ready to meet Linc.

Asher handed Peter's gun to Paige. "You take this one. I'll keep the one Martha left."

"The syringe?"

He patted the pocket of his jacket. "Right here, along with Peter's keys. I can put them back in his pocket. I'm bringing a flashlight this time."

"And there's rope, a knife and tape in the boat-house."

"Everything we need to subdue Linc—and get him talking if we have to."

Paige's eye twitched and he squeezed her shoulder. "Don't worry about it. Leave the rough stuff to me. Remember, I'm a soldier, and as far as I'm concerned, this is war."

Asher locked up the house and killed all the lights except the lamp in the front room, which was on a timer. He locked the back door behind them, and they made their way to the boat dock, holding hands.

Paige laced her fingers with his. "It looks like Preston was right. You haven't had a repeat performance of losing consciousness today. How are you feeling?"

"Seeing Peter rise from the dead and running out here to subdue him worked out the rest of that antidote. I feel fine—so far. But then I felt fine in the coffeehouse just before I slumped in my seat."

"Don't say that." She bumped his shoulder with hers. "If something happens to you during this operation…"

He pressed his finger against her lips. "You'd carry on just fine. I have faith in you to get me out of any scrape."

She puckered her lips and kissed the end of his finger. "Let's do this."

Asher unlocked the boathouse and peeked around the corner. "I wanna make sure Peter hasn't had another resurrection."

Paige flicked the beam from her flashlight over Peter, still stretched out on top of the canvas sheet.

"Keep that light on him." Asher crouched beside the sleeping man and felt his pulse. "He's still alive… and still out."

"Hopefully, he'll stay that way." She aimed the flashlight at the ceiling. "On or off?"

"Linc isn't going to know where the boathouse is and he wouldn't expect Peter to be sitting here in the dark. Leave it on." He checked Peter's phone. "T-minus twenty."

Asher took up his position on one side of the door

and he directed Paige to wait in the back corner. In case this guy came in hot, Asher wanted Paige well away from the door.

Paige drew her gun first. "I'm ready. If you can't bring him down on the first try, I'm going to shoot first and worry about it later."

"I thought you wanted to avoid any unnecessary violence."

"If someone's attacking my man, that's very necessary." She widened her stance like she meant every word.

He liked her new tough swagger—turned him on.

They waited in the semidarkness, every breath they took sounding like a whoosh of air in the stillness of the boathouse.

Asher stole a glance at the phone and then whispered, "Ten minutes."

They didn't have to wait that long. Peter's phone buzzed and Linc's text came through. Asher read it to himself. I'm here.

He flashed the phone at Paige and nodded.

He texted back, Boathouse on the bay shore.

Asher's muscles coiled and his eye twitched. With his foot, he eased open the door, which swung outward.

As Linc left the grass and hit the gravel, Asher could hear every footstep down to the water's edge.

A harsh whisper echoed in the night. "Peter?"

Asher nudged the door again and it creaked on the rusty hinges. He growled, "Over here."

As Linc approached closer…and closer, Asher

curled his fingers around the edge of the door. Then he took a deep breath and pushed the door out.

It met the solid object of Linc's body, and the man grunted.

Asher slammed the door against Linc once more before whipping around and driving his shoulder into the man's midsection.

Linc rocked for a moment like a bowling pin before toppling over.

When Linc hit the ground, Asher dropped to his knees beside him and checked his hands and pockets for weapons. He pulled a gun from Linc's waistband, and a knife from a leg holster. He was collecting quite a stash of weapons. Asher slipped his fingers up Linc's sleeve in case he was carrying a poison pill like Peter had been, but it looked like he was more cowardly than Peter.

Asher rose to his feet and pointed his weapon at the prone man's head. "Don't move. In case you can't see it, I have a gun pointed at you, and in case you didn't feel it, I divested you of all your weapons."

Linc groaned and drew his knees to his chest in a fetal position. "Where's Peter?"

"Crawl into the boathouse and you'll see."

Linc's head jerked up.

"That's right. He's dead. Start crawling or that's gonna be your fate, too."

Asher exchanged a quick look with Paige, who'd ventured outside. Might as well instill some fear into the guy from the get-go.

Linc army-crawled on his belly into the boathouse. His eyes widened when Paige trailed her light across Peter, serenely oblivious to the fact that he was playing possum again.

Linc rolled to his back, and his eyes got even wider. "You're Asher Knight."

"In the flesh."

"You got the jump on Peter? Took his phone?"

"You're a genius." Asher kicked the man's boot. "Now you're going to impart all your knowledge to me. Peter over there wasn't very cooperative."

"Peter doesn't…didn't know anything to tell."

"Too bad for Peter." Asher hunched his shoulders. "I hope you know more."

"Wait, wait." Linc waved his hands in front of his face. "Who's the woman? Is that Tabitha Crane?"

Asher narrowed his eyes. "What do you know about Tabitha?"

"Nothing, nothing."

Paige kept the light away from her face and shrank farther into the corner. If Linc thought she might be the nurse, let him think it.

"If you think Tabitha is here with me, then you must know something about her. What are they saying at Hidden Hills?"

"That she helped you escape. That's how they found you at that cabin. They didn't trust Tabitha and put a GPS tracker on her car. She led them right to you, but we know now there was just one body in that cabin. They were hoping it was yours."

Paige sucked in a breath.

"But then you have your fiancée with you, too,

don't you? Granger and Lewis saw her in that little hick town." Linc snorted. "Before she slipped out of their grasp and they ended up crashing the van. So, which one of your women is this one?"

Asher's jaw tightened. "You seem like you're in a talkative mood. That's good. Keep talking. Who's setting up Major Denver? Who gave the orders to mess with my mind so that I would implicate Denver?"

"Those are some heavy questions."

"I hope you have more answers to them than Peter did."

Linc's eyes rolled sideways to take in his associate. "It's high up. That's all I know. Your amnesia was just one piece in the puzzle—the only piece I know about."

"C'mon, Linc. You can do better than that."

To be more convincing, Asher picked up a pair of pliers and studied them. "You know, even though Delta Force doesn't use torture methods in our operations, it doesn't mean we don't know all about them."

Linc scrambled up to a seated position. "No need, man. Peter and I belong to a web of people who have certain services for hire. That's all. It's not my fight, not my ideology."

"He felt differently." Paige aimed a toe at Peter.

"He's young." Linc shrugged. "Me, I don't care as long as my employers don't think I ratted them out. That's not tolerated. We're even ordered to carry a pill on us, one that simulates death, if we're captured or compromised. Screw that."

"Your employers. Who are they?"

"Wish I could help you with that. I really do, but I take orders from a nameless, faceless text message." He raised one hand. "What I do know is that the setup of Denver goes high up."

"High up where? The military? The government?"

"Both. I think both."

"I need a name, Linc."

"I can't give you a name, but I can give you a hot tip. Can you get the gun out of my face?"

"Gun stays where it is." The man was cooperative, but Asher still didn't trust him. "Let's hear this hot tip."

"The conspiracy against you is laid out in a computer file at Hidden Hills. If you got your hands on that, you could clear your name and come out of hiding."

Asher blew out a breath. Not the bombshell he was expecting.

"Yeah, sure. I can just waltz back into Hidden Hills and ask for my records."

"You might try asking someone else for them."

"The army?" Asher snorted.

"That nurse."

"Tabitha Crane?"

"Yeah, I thought she might be the one standing over there, but now I realize if she was and she really wanted to help you, she'd have given you that file."

Paige asked, "How do you know Tabitha has the file?"

"They all know it now. We have orders to track

her down just like you—and that's the reason. She's become public enemy number two."

"I have a question for you, Linc." Paige stepped from the shadows. "What are you supposed to do with Asher when you find him?"

Linc's gaze darted to the barrel of the gun and back to Paige's face. "Kill him."

The wooden wall across from Asher splintered. Cold air rushed into the boathouse.

Asher lunged in front of Paige and grabbed her hand, yanking her to the floor.

"Get down! They're shooting the place up."

Chapter Fifteen

When Asher had pulled her down, he covered her body with his as the bullets rained above them.

She squirmed beneath him. "Asher, I can't breathe."

He rolled off her and leveled a finger at Linc cowering in the corner. "Did you bring them here? Did you know?"

"No, no. I swear."

"Leave him, Asher."

"His bosses are not going to be as generous as I was." Asher scooted toward the door and kicked it open. "Our only chance now is Peter's boat. Those shots are coming from the house. Follow me."

Paige gritted her teeth as Asher crawled outside. Every cell in her body was screaming, but she pushed past her fear.

When she joined him on the short dock, he shocked her by pushing her off. She rolled into the small powerboat, even as another wall of the boathouse ripped open.

Asher jumped in next to her, flattening himself on

the deck of the boat. He jammed the key into the ignition and pulled on the throttle. The engine roared, churning up the frigid water of the bay.

The boat leaped forward and Paige's head banged against the side.

"Hold on, Paige. I don't know where I'm going and I can't see anything. I don't want to put on the lights until we're farther along."

The boat skimmed across the water, away from the shore, away from the bullets. Paige rubbed her head, tracing the knot already forming there.

After several minutes, the boat's course evened out and Paige realized Asher was upright at the helm.

She dragged herself up, leaning against the inside of the boat, still holding her hand to her head and feeling slightly nauseated, which had nothing to do with seasickness.

Asher's head jerked to the side. "Are you okay? My God, were you hit?"

"No. My head banged against the side of the boat during our escape." She squinted at the distant lights on the shore. "We did escape, didn't we? We got away?"

"We did."

"Y-you weren't shot, were you?"

"No."

"I'm glad you held on to Peter's keys instead of putting them back in his pocket." Paige covered her eyes with one hand. "But all our plans—the car, our clothes, the money—all gone. We're back to square one."

"We're alive." He stretched his hand out to her. "And you're with me."

She wrapped her fingers around his. "You remember me, remember our engagement, remember all the ugliness and you're still here."

"Where else would I be?" He brought her hand to his lips and kissed the tips of her fingers. "I don't know. Square one feels good to me."

His words created a warm bubble around her, and she just wanted to float in that bubble, but they weren't in the floating stage yet.

"Do you think Linc knew he was walking into a trap? He didn't act like it."

"Maybe he was told to play along. He did seem accommodating, but I just had him pegged as a coward." Asher eased off the throttle and the boat's nose lowered in the water. "Or maybe his employers were tracking the phones and noted the unusual activity. Linc looked as surprised as I felt when the bullets started flying."

"Maybe he figured the cavalry coming to rescue him would at least wait until he was out of the way before starting to blast away."

"There's little honor among thieves—another lesson I learned at my father's knee."

"Do you think Linc was telling the truth about your file and Tabitha stealing it?"

"That part makes sense, doesn't it? Linc might've felt he could tell me the truth because he figured I'd be dead ten minutes later."

"Then we need to get our hands on that file. You

can take it to the army. There might be a few traitors, but I refuse to believe the entire army and Delta Force unit are after Major Denver—unless he's really guilty."

"He's not."

"Showing what the doctors at Hidden Hills tried to do to you will put you back on track, anyway. They wouldn't be able to claim you were crazy or a traitor or AWOL then, could they?"

"Somehow I think sneaking back into Hidden Hills is going to be harder than sneaking out."

"Unless we find Tabitha's copy of the file."

"We could return to her family's cabin and look there. My guess is if she has it, she was planning to use it to blackmail me to bend to her wishes."

Paige huddled into her coat. "I don't recall seeing a computer there. It was probably in her car."

"You still have her phone, right?"

"Which I haven't been able to access yet." Paige tried to snap her cold fingers and gave up. "She might have her email on the phone. Maybe we could get some information from that."

"It can't hurt." Asher pointed to some lights along the shoreline. "We're going to have to get off this bay sometime."

"Where are we going to go and what are we going to do without money?" The reality of their situation punched her in the gut, and she folded her arms across her midsection.

"I wouldn't say we have *no* money." Asher patted the pockets of his jacket. "I didn't want to keep going into the bag in the trunk for cash, so when we were packing up I crammed my pockets with the stuff. We'll be okay."

Paige threw her arms around his neck. "You're right. We're safe for now and we're together. All we need is Ivy to make us whole."

"We'll get there, Paige…and we'll be stronger than ever."

SEVERAL HOURS LATER, after ditching Peter's boat, hitching a ride with a trucker and picking up a pizza, Paige fell across the bed in the dumpy motel they found outside of DC.

"I think I might be too tired to eat—bullets, boats and trucks can do that to a girl." She hoisted herself up on her elbows and watched Asher dig into the pizza. "Another spot of good news is that it doesn't seem like you're going to have a relapse of going into a drugged stupor."

Asher pounded his chest with his fist, a piece of pepperoni pizza in the other hand. "I feel great."

"I texted Martha again about the mayhem at her mother's house, but she hasn't responded. I hope she's okay."

"She wasn't planning to go to the house. I'm sure she's fine." Asher wiped his hands on a napkin and held up a can of soda. "If you're not going to eat any-thing, have something to drink."

"I think I will have a piece." She slid off the edge of the bed and pulled a slice out of the box, pinching off a string of cheese with her finger. "Do you think the men with the guns went into the garage and found our car with all our stuff? My laptop's in there."

"I doubt they wanted to stick around that long. They probably swarmed the boathouse, thinking they killed us or trapped us, and found Linc and Peter instead."

"I wonder if they killed Linc…or Peter for that matter."

"Don't waste your sympathy. Do you think either one of them would've hesitated to kill us if they'd had the chance?"

"Ugh, I don't like this world." Paige dabbed her lips with a napkin and took a swig of soda.

"I know you don't. I'm sorry you're in it." He tossed his crust onto a paper plate. "You should be back in Vegas, safe with Ivy."

"Then who'd be your wingman?" She dug her thumb into her chest. "That's me."

Asher leaned forward and kissed her mouth, the spicy pepperoni on his lips making their connection even hotter. "You are my wingman, but you're much, much more, and I want to finish what we started earlier."

She dropped her pizza and stretched her arms over her head. "I don't know. When we were going to make love this afternoon, you were all juiced up on Preston's magic antidote. This could be a total letdown."

"That other guy today? All strength, no substance." He winked. "Do you trust the tub in this place?"

Her gaze scanned the small, plainly furnished

room. "It ain't the Ritz, but it's clean. I'm down for a bath."

"Allow me." Asher pushed away the pizza box and jumped up from his chair. "I'll get things ready."

"Do you want me to save this pizza? There's no fridge in here."

"When did leftover pizza ever need to be refrigerated?" Asher pulled off his boots and socks, one foot at a time, and padded barefoot into the bathroom.

Paige tossed the used paper plates and napkins in the trash and closed the pizza box. Leaning forward, she flipped the curtains at the window.

The lights of the motel office glowed in modest comparison to the headlights of the cars passing on the highway in the distance. They couldn't have been followed or tracked this time. Asher had ditched Linc's and Peter's phones in the bay, and her own phone was turned off. Only the temp phone was active. She'd turned off Tabitha's, but this place—a motel along a string of them on a busy highway—might be the ideal location to turn it on and start entering passwords again.

As far as she knew, phones could be tracked only generally, pinging the nearest cell tower, which could be miles away.

The water stopped running in the bathroom and Asher shouted. "I'm ready. What are you doing out there, finishing off the pizza?"

"Coming." Paige twitched the curtains back in place and put the temp phone along with Tabitha's on the nightstand.

Pulling her sweater over her head, Paige started humming some striptease music as she sauntered to the bathroom. She stopped in the frame of the door and twirled her sweater around by its arm. "Are you really ready, big boy?"

Asher lowered his naked body in the tub, the steam swirling around him. "It's about time."

She dropped her sweater to the floor, yanked off her camisole and bra, and shimmied out of her jeans and panties.

"Hit the switch. I don't have candles, but at least the muted light from the other room lends a little romance to the atmosphere in here."

She tiptoed to the bathtub. "Where'd you get the bubbles?"

"Dumped half this bottle in the water." He held up a small plastic bottle of shower gel.

She dipped a toe into the water between Asher's raised knees. The tub couldn't accommodate the length of his legs stretched out, but she couldn't imagine they'd be in this little tub that long.

She sat down in the water, and the bubbles crackled around her body. Stretching her legs out as far as she could, she leaned back against Asher's chest, finally skin to skin.

Her head lolled against his chest. "I could fall asleep right here."

"You'd better not." He scooped up some bubbles in the palms of his hands and arranged them over her breasts like a mermaid bikini.

She breathed out. "Nice."

Those hands skimmed down her belly and parted her thighs.

Her head fell to the side and her tongue darted out of her mouth and swept across the warm, soapy flesh of his arm.

His fingers stroked between her legs and she rocked with the sensations flowing through her body, creating little waves in the tub. If he kept touching her like that, they'd create a tidal wave.

She arched her back and planted her hands on his knees, digging her fingernails into his skin. The heat from their bodies seemed to bring the water temperature to boiling.

When her orgasm claimed her, she lifted her hips from the water. The pleasure clawed through her body, and her hips pumped the air with every stab.

Asher slid two fingers inside her, and she shuddered around him before falling back to the water, collapsing against his belly.

The water lapped up the side of the tub and spilled over onto the floor.

Asher nibbled her earlobe and then whispered, "You created a tidal wave."

She rolled over to face him, the water giving her buoyancy. "Now I'm going to create a volcano."

Laughing, he wrapped his arms around her. "Not in here, you're not. If I stay in this tub any longer, I'm gonna get stuck."

"Me first." She straddled him and stood up in the tub, dripping water on his head and chest.

Looking up at her, he said, "This is the best view I've had all day."

"Hope you plan to do more than admire the scenery." She stepped over the edge of the tub and grabbed both towels. "Do you need help getting out?"

He flipped the drain stopper with his toe, shifted to his side and rose from the water like Neptune coming out of the sea.

She shook out his towel and crammed it against his chest. "Meet you in the bedroom."

Strolling to the bedroom, she dried herself and then flipped back the covers on the bed. Maybe they'd actually get to make love this time.

She heard Asher's footfall behind her, and before she could turn, he enfolded her in a hug, pressing his front against her back. "It's been too long. I'm kind of glad Peter interrupted us last time. I feel more like myself now, not hopped up on anything, not waiting for any texts or bad guys to show up on our doorstep."

As he kissed the wet tendrils of hair that clung to the back of her neck, he caressed her breasts. She shivered.

"Are you cold?" He scooped her against his body even tighter.

"A little." She wriggled out of his grasp and flung herself across the bed. "Warm me up."

He stretched out beside her on his side and kissed the bump on the side of her head. "War wounds."

He traced the outlines of her face. "I can't believe I ever forgot this face."

"The mind can do funny things. Why don't you touch the rest of my body to make sure you never forget again?"

With his fingers and tongue, he skimmed her flesh, raising goose bumps and setting fire to her nerve endings at the same time. While he reacquainted himself with her body, her fingers idly played in his hair while her other hand stroked his erection.

By the time his head was level with her toes and his feet rested on the pillow next to her head, he was fully aroused and her heart was thundering in her chest.

She rolled to her side so that Asher's erection plowed between her legs. "I think you've proved that all the drugs are out of your system now. I need you inside me. I've waited long enough for you to remember me, remember you love me, forgive me all over again, and now I have you right where I want you."

He tickled the bottom of her foot and then his head joined hers on the pillow. "Ditto."

He kissed her mouth as he straddled her.

She wrapped her legs around his hips as he entered her, like she never wanted to let him go again.

Their lovemaking fell into the familiar pattern they'd established over their years together, but it contained another quality that she couldn't name. Deeper? More satisfying? More secure? Maybe for the first time with Asher, she didn't feel as if she had something to prove.

When they'd finally slaked their need of each

other, Paige rolled to her side, snuggling into the crook of his body, a perfect fit.

He stroked her from the nape of her neck to her derriere. She stretched, curling her toes against his shins.

"Mmm, all my cares just melted away. It's going to be hard going back to the real world."

"You're like a content cat right now, a kitty cat who's lapped up all the cream."

She giggled. "Is that supposed to be some weird double entendre? Ugh, and I just flashed on Tabitha and her obsession with cats. It probably rivaled her obsession with you."

"Sorry I brought up cats."

A light bulb clicked on in Paige's head and she bolted upright. "Tabitha. Cats."

"I said I was sorry." Asher ran a hand down her arm, but she scrambled over his body to reach the nightstand and Tabitha's phone.

"I got it. I know her password."

She snatched the phone from the bedside table and powered it on. The daunting password prompt glared at her again, but this time it had met its match.

She entered the password that had come to her in a flash and yelped when the phone responded by letting her in.

"You did it." Asher gave her a high five. "What was it, genius?"

She rolled her eyes. "Tabbycat, of course."

Paige's finger trembled as she clicked through to

Tabitha's email. "What's the password for the Wi-Fi in here?"

Asher reached past her and dragged a card from beneath the lamp on the nightstand. "Guest."

"That makes it easy." Paige entered the password and held her breath as Tabitha's phone loaded her emails.

Asher hovered over her shoulder, his hot breath stirring her hair. "Check her texts first to make sure nobody's looking for her yet."

Paige skimmed through the emails once to satisfy herself that no secret files jumped out at her. Tabitha had over four hundred emails downloaded to her phone. Asher was right—it could take her a while to go through those.

She flicked to the texts. "There aren't many. One from a Dr. Evans asking her where she is."

"He's a doctor at Hidden Hills. He's obviously not clued in."

"Are any of them? When Linc saw me at the boathouse, he thought I might be Tabitha."

"Linc didn't know much. Maybe they didn't bother to tell him, and maybe they didn't want to tell the doctors at Hidden Hills, either." Asher rolled from the bed and returned to the bathroom. He called out, "Do you want some clothes in here? It's hard for me to concentrate on Tabitha's texts and emails when you're sitting on the edge of the bed naked."

With a smile, Paige said, "Bring me my camisole and underwear."

"That's almost as sexy as your nudity." He returned to the bedroom and tossed the garments at her. "Anything else?"

"Doesn't look like she had many friends. Not even her parents have texted her over the past few days."

"Why would they? She's supposed to be working. They don't know she was at their cabin and maybe they didn't even see the news about that other cabin."

"Her texts haven't told me a thing. It's not like this shadowy network was sending her texts asking her to return to Hidden Hills...or to return you, if they thought she had you."

"How about the emails?" Asher sauntered to the desk in the room and flipped open the pizza box.

"What are you doing?" She peered at him over the top of Tabitha's phone.

"Sex makes me hungry. Told you this pizza wouldn't go to waste. Do you want some?"

"No, thanks." She held out the phone. "I'm busy here."

"Does she have a lot of emails?"

"Over four hundred."

"Do a search. Search for emails with attachments. That should cut down on the number. Search for Hidden Hills, although she might have a lot from her employer."

"I'll search for attachments. If she forwarded your file to herself, it probably would've been as an attachment and not a link."

Paige entered the search for emails with attachments. "That's better."

Folding her legs beneath her, she brought the

phone close to her face and started scrolling through the emails. "She has several with work-related material here. Maybe that's why she was able to hijack your file without the knowledge of Hidden Hills."

"For a while, but they caught on."

"Only when they realized the depth and scope of her obsession for you spurred her on to assist you in your escape, or at least follow you."

Asher joined her on the bed, bunching a few pillows against the headboard behind him. "That escape was all you, superwoman." He pointed to the phone. "Just like accessing Tabitha's phone."

"I should've figured out that password earlier."

"Stop." He put a finger over her lips. "Don't downplay your success. I'm sure I never would've figured that out. What the hell is a tabby cat, anyway?"

"That's right. You're a dog person. A tabby cat is just a standard orange cat. Her nickname was Tabby and it was on the website. Makes sense to me."

"If you say so."

"Speaking of dogs, Ivy really wants one now."

"She's not afraid anymore?"

"We saw some puppies and now she's…" Paige caught her breath. "I think this is it."

Asher scooted closer to her on the bed. "You found the email? The file?"

"Looks like she tried to disguise the attachment by putting medication notes in the email, but this attachment popped up when I searched for your name."

"Before you even open the attachment, forward it to your own email address, forward it to mine, forward it to your mother's. If I had Cam's personal email memorized, I'd have you forward it to him, too."

"What about someone official in Delta Force?"

"Let's see what the file has in it before we do that. What if it just confirms my accusations against Major Denver? Sending it to Delta Force could just make things worse for him."

"Okay." Paige forwarded Tabitha's email to her own email address, Asher's and Mom's. She'd warned Mom enough times about phishing emails that she just might delete it, so she added a short note indicating herself as the sender and asking her mother to save the email.

"The moment of truth." Paige clicked on the attachment, her eyes glued to the circle spinning on the display as the file downloaded. "I wish I had my laptop."

The file finally opened and Paige enlarged the text on the display. Leaning into Asher's space, she shared the phone with him. "Here it is."

They read it silently, side by side, Asher nodding each time she indicated she wanted to move on.

Asher turned and kissed the side of her head before they'd even finished the file. "You did it. That's it. Proof that the memories were implanted in my mind."

"No explanation of why or on whose orders though."

He tapped the phone. "Not yet. We haven't read it all."

Paige rubbed her eyes. "Not sure I can get through any more. It's been a crazy day. We thought we were going to get some info from Linc and head out with a car packed with food, cash…and my laptop."

"Instead we're here, and my amazing fiancée got us the info we needed to get me back on the right side of the US Army and get us home to Ivy."

She snuggled against Asher, the phone still clutched in her hand. "I can't wait."

He flicked off the light beside her and pulled her close. "Let's get some sleep and figure out where we're going to deliver this file tomorrow. Once it's in the hands of the proper authorities, I'm sure the orders for Hidden Hills will change and we'll no longer be in danger. They're the ones who are going to be in trouble now."

"I'll go to sleep once I get through this file. There's not much more."

Asher yawned. "And I don't think you're going to find anything of importance. The rest just looks like a so-called treatment schedule to me."

Blinking, Paige refocused on the display glowing in the dark and read the rest of the attachment with drooping eyelids. Nothing she read could keep her from falling asleep.

They'd succeeded—she and Asher together.

As light crept through the gap in the drapes, Paige's hand tingled. She flexed her fingers and realized Tabitha's phone was buzzing.

Maybe Tabitha finally got a meaningful text. Paige

squinted at the green digits of the alarm clock and nudged Asher's shoulder. "It's eight o'clock already."

Rolling to her side, she turned on the light and pushed up against the headboard. She entered the password for the phone and tapped the incoming text message from a Dr. Evans.

She read the text once, her head tilted to one side. She read it again, the fog of sleep beginning to clear. Then it cleared all at once to devastating clarity.

She dropped the phone on the floor and doubled over, gasping to get air into her lungs.

"Paige?" Asher gripped her upper arm. "Paige, are you okay?"

She turned to face him, her lips trying to form the words that would destroy his world. She'd failed him again.

"Paige? What's wrong?"

"They took Ivy."

Chapter Sixteen

Asher stared at Paige's pale face, her mouth still hanging open after delivering the nonsensical words.

"What are you talking about? Ivy's with your mom in Vegas."

"N-no, she's not. They have her. The people who are still after us have taken our daughter."

One part of Asher's mind shut down. Another part began manufacturing denials.

He snorted. "How would you know that? Your mother's not in contact with you. Nobody is."

She dipped her chin. "They contacted Tabitha, or rather they contacted me through Tabitha's phone. Ivy's gone."

Fear galloped through Asher's body and he leaped from the bed and fell to the floor on Paige's side of the bed. He grabbed the phone that had been the source of so much satisfaction only hours before.

He tapped the text and read it aloud. "'We have your daughter. Any moves from you and you'll never see her again.'"

A sob broke from Paige's throat and white-hot

COMING NEXT MONTH FROM

H HARLEQUIN®

INTRIGUE

Available December 18, 2018

YOU CAN FIND MORE INFORMATION ON UPCOMING HARLEQUIN® TITLES, FREE EXCERPTS AND MORE AT WWW.HARLEQUIN.COM.

HICNM1218

SPECIAL EXCERPT FROM

HQN™

*When Ashley Jo "AJ" Somerfield is told that
Cyrus Cahill is missing and presumed dead,
she refuses to believe the worst. Now she will
do whatever it takes to bring him home.*

Read on for a sneak preview of
Wrangler's Rescue,
*the final book in The Montana Cahills series
by* New York Times *bestselling author B.J. Daniels.*

Ashley Jo "AJ" Somerfield couldn't help herself. She kept looking
out the window of the Stagecoach Saloon hoping to see a familiar
ranch pickup. Cyrus Cahill had promised to stop by as soon as
he returned to Gilt Edge. He'd been gone less than a week after
driving down to Denver to see about buying a bull for the ranch.

"I'll be back on Saturday," he'd said when he left. "Isn't that the
day Billie Dee makes chicken and dumplings?"

He knew darned well it was. "Texas chicken and dumplings,"
AJ had corrected him, since everything Billie Dee cooked had
a little of her Southern spice in it. "I know you can't resist her
cookin' so I guess I'll see you then."

He'd laughed. Oh, how she loved that laugh. "Maybe you will
if you just happen to be tending bar on Saturday."

"I will be." That was something else he knew darned well.

He'd let out a whistle. "Then I guess I'll see you then."

She smiled to herself at the memory. It had taken Cyrus a while
to come out of his shell. One of those "aw shucks, ma'am" kind
of cowboys, he was so darned shy she thought she was going to
have to throw herself on the floor at his boots for him to notice her.
But once he had opened up a little, they'd started talking, joking
around, getting to know each other.

PHEXPBJD1218

Before he'd left, they'd gone for a horseback ride through the snowy foothills up into the towering pines of the forest. It had been Cyrus's idea. They'd ridden up into one of the four mountain ranges that surrounded the town of Gilt Edge—and the Cahill Ranch.

It was when they'd stopped to admire the view from the mountaintop that overlooked the small western town that AJ had hoped Cyrus would kiss her. He sure looked as if he'd wanted to as they'd walked their horses to the edge of the overlook.

The sun warming them while the breeze whispered through the boughs of the snow-laden nearby pines, it was one of those priceless Montana January days between snowstorms. That was why Cyrus had said they should take advantage of the beautiful day before he left for Denver.

Standing on a bared-off spot on the edge of the mountain, he'd reached over and taken her hand in his. "Beautiful," he'd said. For a moment she thought he was talking about the view, but when she met his gaze she'd seen that he'd meant her.

Her heart had begun to pound. This was it. This was what she'd been hoping for. He drew her closer. Pushing back his Stetson, he bent toward her. His mouth was just a breath away from hers—when his mare nudged him with her nose.

She could laugh about it now. But if she hadn't grabbed Cyrus he would have fallen down the mountainside.

"She's just jealous," Cyrus had said of his horse as he'd rubbed the beast's neck after getting his footing under himself again.

But the moment had been lost. They'd saddled up and ridden back to Cahill Ranch.

AJ still wanted that kiss more than anything. Maybe today when Cyrus returned home. After all, it had been his idea to stop by the saloon his brother and sister owned when he got back. She thought it wasn't just Billie Dee's chicken and dumplings he was after, and bit her lower lip in anticipation.

Don't miss
Wrangler's Rescue *by B.J. Daniels,*
available December 2018 wherever
Harlequin® *books and ebooks are sold.*

www.Harlequin.com

Get 4 FREE REWARDS!

We'll send you 2 FREE Books <u>plus</u> 2 FREE Mystery Gifts.

Harlequin Intrigue® books feature heroes and heroines that confront and survive danger while finding themselves irresistibly drawn to one another.

FREE Value Over $20

I N T R I G U E

*When navy SEAL Trace "T-Mac" McGuire is tasked
with protecting a sexy dog handler, Kinsley Anderson,
and her uniquely trained dog, he never imagines
he will fall for her. As their search for a traitor selling
arms to Somalian rebels places them in increasingly
dangerous situations, can T-Mac keep
Kinsley—and his heart—safe?*

Read on for a sneak preview of
Six Minutes to Midnight
by New York Times bestselling author Elle James.

"Four days and a wake-up," Trace McGuire, T-Mac to
his friends, said as he sat across the table in the chow
hall on Camp Lemonnier. They'd returned from their
last mission in Niger with news they were scheduled to
redeploy back to the States.

He glanced around the table at his friends. When they
were deployed, they spent practically every waking hour
together. In the past, being stateside was about the same.
They'd go to work, train, get briefed, work out and then
go back to their apartments. Most of the time, they'd end
up at one of the team members' places to watch football,
cook out, or just lounge around and shoot the crap with
each other. They were like family and never seemed to
get tired of each other's company.

T-Mac suspected all that was about to change. All of
his closest SEAL buddies had women in their lives now.
All except him. Suddenly, going back to Virginia wasn't

quite as appealing as it had been in the past. T-Mac sighed and drank his lukewarm coffee.

"I can't wait to see Reese." Diesel tapped a finger against the rim of his coffee cup. "I promised to take her on a real date when I get back to civilization."

"What? You're not going to take her swinging through the jungle, communing with the gorillas?" Buck teased.

Petty Officer Dalton Samuel Landon, otherwise known as Diesel, shook his head. "Nope. Been there, done that. I think I'll take her to a restaurant where we don't have to forage for food. Then maybe we'll go out to a nightclub." He tipped his head to the side. "I wonder if she likes to dance."

"You mean you don't know?" Big Jake Schuler, the tallest man on the team, rolled his eyes. "I would have thought that in the time you two spent traipsing along the Congo River, you would know everything there was to know about each other."

Diesel frowned. "I know what's important. She's not fragile, she can climb a tree when she needs to, she doesn't fall apart when someone's shooting at her and she can kiss like nobody's business." Diesel shrugged. "In fact, I'm looking forward to learning more. She's amazing. How many female bodyguards do you know?"

Big Jake held up his hands in surrender. "You got me there. None."

Don't miss
Six Minutes to Midnight *by Elle James,*
available January 2019 wherever
Harlequin® *Intrigue books and ebooks are sold.*

www.Harlequin.com

Need an adrenaline rush from nail-biting tales
(and irresistible males)?

Check out **Harlequin Intrigue®**
and **Harlequin® Romantic Suspense** books!

New books available every month!

CONNECT WITH US AT:

Facebook.com/groups/HarlequinConnection

Facebook.com/HarlequinBooks

Twitter.com/HarlequinBooks

Instagram.com/HarlequinBooks

Pinterest.com/HarlequinBooks

ReaderService.com

 **HARLEQUIN®**

**ROMANCE WHEN
YOU NEED IT**

SGENRE2018

rage thumped through Asher's body. He sat on the edge of the bed, and she collapsed against his chest.

"We don't even know if this is true, Paige. They could be lying."

"There's one way to find out." She reached for the other phone on the nightstand, the one they'd kept powered down for fear of being tracked.

Paige tapped the display. Her body stiffened and she choked out more words he didn't want to hear. "Oh my God. I have about twenty texts from my mother—Ivy's gone."

Asher caught Paige as she began to slump forward. "It's going to be okay, Paige. I'll make it okay. I'll give them whatever they want to keep Ivy safe. What does your mother say?"

He pried the phone from Paige's stiff fingers and read through Cheryl's texts, each one more frantic than the previous one. "They've ordered your mother to keep silent, and it looks like she's complied so far. Call her."

Paige stared at the phone in his hand, her bottom lip trembling. Then she snatched it from him and made the call.

Asher reached over and put the phone on speaker as it rang.

Cheryl picked up before the first ring ended. "Oh my God, Paige. Where have you been? Somebody kidnapped Ivy and I think it has to do with whatever is going on with you and Asher."

Paige took a long shuddering breath and drew

back her shoulders. "It does, Mom. What do they want you to do?"

"Me?" Her mother's voice cracked and it took her several seconds to continue. "Nothing, nothing at all—no police, no FBI, no Terrence. I haven't even told Terrence, who's off somewhere hiking. They want you and Asher. They want to make some kind of deal with him."

Asher rubbed a circle on Paige's ramrod-straight back. "Don't worry, Cheryl. I'm going to get her back. I'll give them what they want."

"What do they want, Asher?"

"Me. They want me."

"They're not going to get you." Paige flicked back her messy hair and clenched her jaw.

"Paige." Her mother sniffled. "Let Asher handle it. This is Ivy we're talking about. Of course Asher's going to do whatever it takes to save her."

"They're not going to get Asher, and they're not going to keep Ivy. They have no idea what they walked into. They've just made a big mistake."

Asher massaged Paige's neck. He knew she'd turned into a fierce lioness when it came to Ivy, but he didn't see any other way out. He'd have to forget about his Hidden Hills file and let them use him to help bring down Major Denver. Just as long as they sent Ivy home to her mother.

Cheryl choked out, "Paige, I've done everything they've asked of me, even keeping this from Terrence. Now it's your turn. You and Asher have to follow their orders to protect Ivy."

"Don't worry about a thing, Mom. We'll rescue her. When are you expecting Terrence?"

"He'll be gone for another few days. If he were here, there's no way I could hide this from him."

"Good. Just keep doing what you're doing. I'll let you know when we have Ivy." Paige ended the call with her mother and turned to Asher, her eyes wide, her lips parted, her breath coming out in short spurts.

Asher took both of her hands. "What do you have in mind, Paige? I don't plan to make any moves until Ivy is home safe, and then I swear I'll make them all pay."

"We can find her, Asher. We can get Ivy back and you don't have to surrender yourself."

"I don't see how that's going to happen, Paige. We know nothing about these people. We don't have any idea what they've done with Ivy."

"Not yet." Paige slipped her hands from his and grabbed his shoulders. "As soon as I get my hands on a computer, we'll know exactly where they're keeping Ivy—because I had her microchipped."

He jerked back from her. "You did what?"

"I had Ivy microchipped when she was a baby— the first time you left me alone with her."

"Why would you do that? Is it even legal?"

"Elena's ex-boyfriend, the doctor, he did it for me. As to why…" She hunched her shoulders. "You know why. I was afraid, afraid I'd lose her again. I didn't want to tell you or my mom I'd done it. It wasn't going to be forever."

The enormity of Paige's confession flooded his

senses all at once and he grabbed her face and planted a kiss on her mouth. "Finally your self-flagellation over your sins resulted in some good. You're amazing. You must've known this day was coming."

Paige blinked her eyes. "I-it is amazing, isn't it? We're going to be able to pinpoint Ivy's location without their knowledge—I just need a computer. I have a log-in to the website, and we'll be able to track her from that."

"If the service has a website, they must have an app for your phone. Have you ever tried that?"

"I've never even used the service, Asher. I hope it works."

He swept up her phone from the floor where she'd dropped it. "Do a search. Do you remember the name of the service?"

"Of course. KidFinder." She took the phone in her hand and froze. "Tabitha's phone is going off. It's a phone call."

"Let me." He picked up the call. "Yeah?"

"Lieutenant Knight himself. Memories all back in place, I presume?"

"Enough to know I was used to set up Major Denver. Why?"

"Tsk, tsk, Knight. Don't we have more important issues to settle? You must've verified by now that we have your daughter."

"Verified, but how do we know she's okay?"

"I'll have her…caretakers do a face-to-face session for you on the phone, this phone, and then you'll do as we say."

"You want me to go back to my original false story about what happened during that meeting with Denver and his contact."

The voice hardened. "We want you back at Hidden Hills, under our control."

Paige stiffened beside him.

"Who are you? Who are you working for? What do you have against Denver?"

"Maybe all will be revealed when you join us."

"We need our daughter back with us before I go anywhere."

"Understood. We'll do a trade."

"Where?"

"Las Vegas—she's not far from there. We weren't going to try to get her on an airplane. We'll give you a location for the trade…when you get here. You and Paige will come together. We'll send your lovely fiancée off with your daughter, and we'll take you back to Hidden Hills."

"What's to stop me from escaping again or turning on you once we have our daughter back?"

Paige punched his thigh, and he put a finger to his lips.

"You won't have that opportunity ever again, Knight."

Paige's fingers had uncurled on his leg, and now her nails dug into his flesh.

Asher understood. Once he served his usefulness to the cause, he'd commit suicide or have some other kind of accident.

"And what reassurances can you give me that my

daughter and my fiancée won't be in danger from you again?"

"Why would we want to harm them? We'll get what we want from you, and once we do, your family will never hear from us again. We don't like exposing ourselves in this way—unless it's absolutely necessary."

Sounded like a pretty good deal to him—except the part where he'd have to die.

"How are we going to get to Vegas? I don't have my ID, my wallet, nothing."

"We'll get those back to you, and we'll give you the day, time and location of the meeting place."

"I'm not coming anywhere near you until my daughter is safe."

"Tell us how to get your belongings to you and we'll deliver them."

"Leave them at the front desk of the Ambassador Hotel in DC, near Dulles. I'll make sure I get them."

"It seems that we're all on the same page now, Knight. We'll have your possessions waiting for you at the Ambassador by five o'clock tonight. Be in Vegas by ten o'clock tomorrow night and we'll text you the location for the trade."

"We'll be there. If anything happens to our daughter in the meantime, I'll blow your plans sky-high."

The man on the other end of the line chuckled. "I doubt that, Knight. You do know that Nurse Tabitha Crane is no longer around to help you."

"She wasn't much help."

"Then you won't miss her, either."

The man cut off the call before Asher could even respond. It was just as well if nobody suspected he had his file from Hidden Hills. If their rescue of Ivy didn't go as planned before the trade, Paige didn't need the specter of that file hanging over her.

Almost immediately after that call ended, another came through.

Paige tugged on his sleeve. "It might be Ivy."

It was. As soon as Asher accepted the call, his daughter's sweet face filled the display. A golf ball–sized lump formed in his throat and his eyes stung with tears.

"Hey there, Ivy."

"Daddy!"

"Mommy's here, too."

Paige leaned her head against Asher's. "How are you, little bunny? Are you having fun?"

Ivy's face slipped away, replaced by a blank wall and a hushed voice. "That's enough. She's alive, healthy and will be waiting for you tomorrow."

Asher's eyes burned after the call ended and the image disappeared. He tossed Tabitha's phone onto the bed. "They plan to kill me. You know that, right? They'll use me to bolster their story, and then I'm done."

"When did you become such a pessimist?" Paige held up her phone and tilted it back and forth. "Not only did I find the app on my phone, I successfully logged in and I located Ivy—she's at Circus Circus. They just made a big mistake."

Asher curled his hand for a fist bump and Paige touched her knuckles to his.

"Vegas, baby. That's *our* town."

Chapter Seventeen

Paige grabbed Asher's hand as they stepped outside of McCarran International Airport. The high desert had a chill in the air, but the dry breeze made her feel right at home. She'd be able to shed the winter jacket if not the sweater.

They weren't going to stay with Mom or anywhere near her. They'd checked the KidFinder app as soon as they got off the red-eye from DC to verify that Ivy was still at the Circus Circus Hotel & Casino.

Paige grabbed Asher's arm as they settled into the back of a taxi. "You're sure Frankie Greco can help us?"

"Frankie the Greek and my dad go way back. Even though the Greek is retired from the mob, he still has his Vegas connections. All the hotel owners are legit now, but they still owe Frankie and Frankie owes my dad." Asher kissed the back of her hand. "Are you sure your ladies of the night can help us?"

"I've seen more hookers than all the politicians in DC have, and I've signed off on their court orders even when they missed a few sessions. They'll help us if we need it."

"We've got mobsters and hookers on our side in Vegas. How can we miss?"

Paige glanced at the rearview mirror and whispered, "I hope they didn't harm that kid we sent into the Ambassador to pick up your stuff."

"Why would they? I don't think there's any way they could've followed him, especially not on that skateboard he took through the metro station. They just want me here in Vegas so they can do the trade and get me back on track at Hidden Hills. They're not expecting any surprises from us."

"Boy, do we have some surprises for them."

The taxi dropped them off at the hotel-casino next to Circus Circus. Paige's mom had made the reservations for them with Terrence's credit card and pre-paid for the room.

By the time they checked in and got settled it was one o'clock in the morning. Asher had already made contact with the old mobster Frankie Greco, and he'd agreed to meet with them for breakfast.

Paige plucked the sweater from her midsection. "I don't know about you, but I'm getting an early start tomorrow and going shopping for an outfit. I'm sick of this sweater and these dirty jeans."

"I'll join you. We need to get a good night's sleep. It's gonna be a busy day tomorrow."

THE FOLLOWING MORNING, Paige turned on her phone just long enough to check the app. Ivy's GPS was accurate enough to pinpoint the wing of the hotel room where she was located. "They're still at Circus Circus."

"I hope they don't plan to move Ivy hours before the meeting. For all we know, they could decide to do the trade out in the desert somewhere and make a move early."

"Then the sooner we put our plan in motion, the better. I still don't understand how Frankie is going to be able to get all the guests out of Circus Circus."

"If anyone can get results in this town, it's Frankie."

An hour later, dressed in a pair of jeans with silver studs around the pockets and a top with a few too many sequins, Paige slid into a banquette across from Asher in one of the many restaurants in their hotel.

Frankie entered a few minutes after they sat down and caused a commotion as he made his way to their table—smiles, pats on the back and waves across the room.

Paige rolled her eyes at Asher. "He really is Mr. Vegas, isn't he?"

"And he's on our side." Asher nudged her out of the booth and greeted the stubby, balding man who looked more like someone's grandpa than a feared mobster. He gave the man a one-armed hug. "Thanks for meeting us, Frankie."

Frankie the Greek collapsed in the seat across from them, huffing out a breath. "When someone takes a kid, the gloves are off."

They didn't have to explain to him why these people had taken Ivy, who they were or why they hadn't involved the authorities. A guy like Frankie the Greek operated outside the boundaries of the law.

As soon as Frankie sat at their table, the waitress materialized as if by magic and took their orders. "You and your friends can order whatever you like, Frankie. The boss says it's on the house."

"Glenn may regret that, sweetheart. I'm as hungry as a bear and twice as fierce." He winked at the waitress, who blew him a kiss.

Paige slid a glance at Asher. The guy had it made in this town.

When the waitress left, Frankie hunched over the table, blinking his bulging frog-like eyes. "So, they got her at the Circus Circus? I have my contacts there. Do you know which room?"

Asher shook his head. "We know the wing, but not the floor or the room."

"I can change that." He leveled a finger at Paige. "You got a picture of the little angel?"

Paige scrambled for her phone and pulled up a recent picture of Ivy.

"Send that to me, sweetheart. You know what the perps look like?"

Paige shoved her phone to Asher so that he could send the picture to Frankie. "We don't have the slightest idea."

Frankie peppered them with more questions, like when they would've checked in and did they know what Ivy was wearing. Unless the kidnappers had bought her additional clothes, Ivy would be wearing what she had on during their video chat yesterday.

When Frankie had exhausted all his questions, he slurped some coffee from his cup. "I'll tell ya what I'm gonna do. I'm gonna get some people to go through the security footage at the hotel and locate your little girl. We're gonna get her exact room number."

"W-we have to get her out by at least nine o'clock tonight." Paige folded her hands on the table in front of her, and her engagement ring cut into her flesh.

"Don't worry, sweetheart." Frankie patted her clenched hands. "I'll get an army of people on this. We'll find her."

Asher draped his arm around Paige. "Then what, Frankie? Storm the room? We don't want to endanger Ivy."

Frankie spread his arms. "What do I look like? An amateur?"

He laid out the plan for them, arranged to have a gun delivered to their room for Asher and then ordered a second helping of hash browns. "The more distractions we have in that hallway, the better."

"I have some…friends I can call on." Paige crumpled her napkin next to her plate of food, which she'd hardly touched. "Thanks for breakfast, Frankie. Thanks for everything."

"You kids get lost until game time." He shoved a wad of cash toward Asher. "Treat your girl to a little spa action, Asher."

Asher held out his hand. "I can't take that, Frankie."

The old mobster puffed out his cheeks. "Do it for an old man. I owe your father."

Asher swept the cash off the table and into his pocket. "If we get Ivy back safe and sound, all debts to my father will be paid in full."

Frankie waved his hand and secured his napkin under his chin before diving into his potatoes and peppers.

When they got to the room, Paige perched on the edge of the bed, pinning her hands between her knees. "Do you think it's going to work?"

"It has to." He thumbed the stack of bills in her direction. "How about it? You want to hit up the spa?"

"You're kidding." She fell back on the bed. "I wanna throw up."

He tossed the money at her. "No time for that. You need to call your girls in and give them their marching orders."

She clapped the money to her chest. "Are you suggesting I'm going to have to pay them to help me out?"

"Well, they *are* hookers."

"They're hookers with hearts of gold, and most have kids of their own."

"Then maybe I'll get the spa treatment."

LATER THAT AFTERNOON, the call came and Asher wiped his hands on the thighs of his jeans before answering Tabitha's phone and putting it on speaker for Paige. "Yeah? Took you long enough."

The familiar, hated voice purred over the line. "You in Vegas?"

"We are. Where do you want us for the meeting?"

"We'll pick you up."

Paige poked his leg, shaking her head.

"I thought we were meeting you somewhere."

"You thought wrong, Lieutenant. We'll give you a location and we'll send a car to get you."

"I'm not getting into any car with anyone until Paige has our daughter."

"We'll be bringing your daughter with us in the car. She's very excited about riding in a limousine. We'll pick up you and Paige. You can verify the safety of your daughter, and then we'll drop off Paige and the little girl…and you're ours. And we'd better not see any information surface about our operation or the activities at Hidden Hills."

"We don't know anything."

"Right. Here's what you're going to do."

He gave them the time and location for the pickup, and Asher let out a long, silent breath. They still had plenty of time to put their own plan into action.

"We'll be there."

"Remember, no weapons, no police, no trackers, nobody following us. All those things would be very, very bad for your family, Lieutenant."

"Got it."

Asher turned off the phone and cupped it in his hands. Then he kissed Paige hard on the mouth.

"He didn't say anything about old mobsters and hookers, did he?"

Four hours after that phone call and three hours before the scheduled meeting time, Asher stashed the gun, which Frankie had sent over, in his pocket.

"Are you ready?"

Paige squared her shoulders as if heading into battle—which wasn't too far off the mark. "I'm ready. What if they see us? Recognize us?"

"How? Even if they have lookouts, which seems unlikely as there's no reason for them to suspect we know they're even at a hotel in Vegas, let alone *that* hotel, we have some pretty good disguises." Asher stroked the beard covering the lower half of his face and tugged the baseball cap over his forehead.

Paige smoothed the short, sparkly dress over her thighs and tousled her dark pixie-cut wig. "I don't think I'd even recognize you in that getup."

"And Krystal packed enough makeup on your face to practically change the shape."

"It's called contouring, and Krystal's trying to leave the life to go legit as a makeup artist."

"She could use you in her portfolio." He put his hand on the small of her back as he steered her out of the room. "Now let's go rescue our daughter."

They reached the Circus Circus Hotel & Casino just as a circus act was starting, which had brought in more people and created more activity.

Asher whispered in Paige's ear, "The more chaos, the better."

They took the elevator up to the tenth floor of the

hotel, and Asher could almost feel the tugging at his heartstrings the closer he got to his daughter.

When they reached the tenth floor, they got off the elevator and headed for the stairwell. They climbed up two flights of stairs to the twelfth floor.

Asher paused, his hand on the handle of the fire door. "Are you ready?"

"Oh, yeah."

They slipped through the door onto the twelfth floor and sidled along the wall to the vending area. Almost immediately, a swarm of hotel personnel, courtesy of Frankie the Greek, fanned out along the floor and began knocking on doors.

"Evacuation. This is an evacuation. Everyone out of the rooms and into the stairwells."

Guests began opening their doors and grumbling or shouting. Asher kept his eye on one door only.

He held his breath as a hotel employee banged on that door. "Evacuation. Everyone out."

People began streaming down the hallway, jostling each other to reach the stairwell doors. Frankie had picked the perfect time—right between daytime activities and dinner and gambling. Most people were back in their rooms getting ready for their nighttime plans.

Paige's brigade of helpful hookers further clogged the hallway and did their best to push people along and create more distractions.

Asher elbowed Paige as the door to Ivy's cell inched open. A woman poked her head into the hallway and then called back over her shoulder. A man joined her at the door, and then it slammed shut.

Asher's heart slammed with it.

Paige hissed, "They can't stay in there, right? They're going to have to come out with everyone else."

"If they don't, we'll send in one of Frankie's guys to get them."

The door swung open again, and Paige clutched his arm as the couple appeared in the frame, the man holding Ivy in his arms.

As soon as they stepped into the hallway, Paige's friends began to march toward them, chattering and grabbing on to other guests.

As the man carrying Ivy moved down the hallway, Asher's gaze dropped to the right hand he kept in one pocket—most likely curled around the handle of a gun.

The couple passed Asher and Paige without a second look, and they stepped into the hallway behind them. Ivy looked over the man's shoulder and met Asher's eyes.

Asher looked away, his muscles coiled, but the danger passed. His daughter had never seen him with a beard before in her young life.

A clump of people shuffled to the fire door, but everyone had to wait their turn. Two of the women in Krystal's crew swooped in on the man who had Ivy.

"Ooh, is this your little family?" One of the women stationed herself in front of the man, while the other pushed up against the woman.

The man jerked back. "Who the hell are you? Get outta my way, you whore."

The woman confronting him waved a finger in his face. "That's no way to talk in front of your daughter. That's also no way to talk in front of the woman you were cuddling up to last night."

"I don't know what you're talking about. Get outta my face." The man's hand hovered at his pocket.

The other woman took Ivy's hand. "Hello, sweetie. Your daddy is a bad boy, isn't he?"

"What the hell?" The man shoved the woman against the wall, but his grip on Ivy loosened.

His companion took over and pulled Ivy from his arms.

Paige stiffened beside Asher and growled, "You take care of him. I'll get our daughter."

Asher tried to grab Paige's arm to stop her, but it was no use. He turned his attention to the man, and as soon as Ivy left his arms for the woman's, Asher charged and punched the man in the kidney.

He choked and staggered forward, reaching for his gun.

Asher had his out first and slammed the butt of his against the man's skull. Blood spurted from his scalp as he fell to the floor.

The scuffle beside him had Asher spinning around—just in time to see Paige smash her fist into the side of the woman's face.

"That's *my* daughter, bitch."

Epilogue

Asher put a finger to his lips as Ivy crawled over his legs singing, "London bridges, London bridges, London bridges."

Paige swooped in and scooped up her daughter. "Shh. Daddy's on the phone."

She carried Ivy into the kitchen, where her mother and Terrence were drinking coffee.

"I don't know why you didn't call me as soon as Ivy…" Terrence glanced at Ivy's blond curls bobbing in time to the song she was singing. "You know."

"They told me not to, Terrence." Mom stirred some cream into her coffee. "You would've gone in there with guns blazing. I knew Asher…and Paige could handle it."

Asher joined them in the kitchen, pocketing his phone. "We handled the most important part, but the army still refuses to exonerate Major Denver. Said there's still too much evidence tying him to that terrorist group to clear his name."

"But your name is cleared, right?" Paige wrapped

her arms around his waist. "Is that what the phone call was about?"

"Let's take this in the other room." Asher ruffled Ivy's hair.

Mom pushed back from the table. "Ivy, do you want to go to the park across the street with me and Terrence?"

Ivy curled one arm around Asher's leg. "Is Daddy going away?"

Asher hoisted Ivy into his arms. "I'll be here through Christmas. Are you going to stay awake so we can look at the Christmas lights tonight?"

"Daddy, can we have hot chocolate after?" She patted his face as if to make sure he didn't have that beard that had scared her the night of her rescue.

"Of course. What are Christmas lights without hot chocolate after?"

"With marshmallows?"

"Hmm." Asher raised his eyes to the ceiling. "I think we can find some marshmallows."

Paige leaned over Asher's shoulder and kissed Ivy on the tip of her turned-up nose. "As long as we can have whipped cream, too."

"Marshmallows *and* whipped cream." Asher set Ivy on the floor. "Now go with Grandma and Terrence. Mommy and I will be over in a minute."

When Terrence and Mom took Ivy out the front door, Paige still felt a chill race up her spine. Would she ever feel comfortable allowing Ivy out of her sight? She still had her chip, but she and Asher had agreed to have it removed.

They didn't have anything to fear from the conspirators at Hidden Hills anymore. Asher had turned over his Hidden Hills file to a commanding officer in Delta Force and army personnel had moved into Hidden Hills and closed it down.

Asher slumped in a chair at the dining room table. "I'm all clear, Paige. They believe my story because it's all there in the file from Hidden Hills, but the doctors who engineered my brainwashing refused to implicate anyone else. They took the fall themselves and claimed they were conducting unauthorized experiments."

"And the kidnappers refused to talk."

"I don't see how that woman *could* talk after you clocked her in the jaw." Asher winked. "That was awesome."

Her lips twisted into a smile. "That did feel pretty good, but they haven't said anything about who gave them the orders to take Ivy or why."

"They pretended it was all a part of the Hidden Hills experiments."

"Does the army really believe that?"

"I don't think so, but nobody is talking. Nobody is cracking." Asher slammed his fist on the table. "What more do they want? Cam and Martha proved that the emails that started the whole investigation into Denver were bogus, and we just shot holes in the narrative that Denver killed an army ranger and tried to kill me while meeting with a known terrorist. What more do they want?"

"There's more to his story, isn't there? Why

doesn't he come in? Why doesn't he surrender and try to prove his innocence?"

"If I know Major Denver, he'll do that on his own terms and only when he has a handle on who tried to set him up."

"He may never come in." Paige slid into Asher's lap. "But you're safe? We're safe?"

"There's no reason for anyone to come after us now. I'm out of their clutches, and the file that Tabitha stole implicates everyone at Hidden Hills. That so-called rehabilitation center is now closed and will reopen with new staff."

"Is someone going to face murder charges for Tabitha's death?"

"I guess we'll see who decides to take the fall for that. So far there's a lot of finger-pointing going on with nobody taking full responsibility."

"That's because nobody at Hidden Hills *is* fully responsible. They were following someone else's orders, and it doesn't look like we'll ever find out who's behind the conspiracy."

"Oh, we're gonna find out." He kissed the side of her head. "Why were we waiting to get married? I must've never recovered that memory."

"I just wanted to make sure..." She trailed off and rested her cheek against his hair.

"That I forgave you? Trusted you? Wanted you to be the mother of all the rest of my children?"

"The rest?"

He tucked his arm around her waist. "We both

hated being only children, didn't we? I'm not putting Ivy through that. She's going to have a few siblings."

"A few?"

"Ivy's got the greatest mom in the world. It's only right she share her with some brothers and sisters."

Tears pooled in Paige's eyes and she cupped Asher's strong jaw with one hand. "And all I had to do was save you from a psychiatric prison and rescue Ivy from a couple of kidnappers to prove it."

"Paige, you never had to prove anything to me. Your love was always enough…and it always will be. Christmas wedding?"

"Are you serious?"

"Why not? We *are* in Vegas."

"Just as long as we don't have an Elvis impersonator performing the ceremony."

"You're no fun. Let's go tell Ivy—and we don't need a microchip to find her." Asher pounded a fist against his chest over his heart. "You're both always right here with me."

* * * * *